W9-CPM-536

In these twenty-seven tales, men and women from all walks of life—nobles, soldiers, hunters and peasants—are faced with threats to their lives and freedom. Their adversary may be human or demon, the danger physical or spiritual, but each character must—and usually does—prove himself against the foe.

Maui, in the title story, has cunning and courage enough to defy the gods, gaining for mankind the precious gift of fire. Like him, Vassilissa, Onkoito, Prince Five-Weapons, and all the others bravely face their enemies.

Using intellect as well as strength to meet the challenge, the heroes and rebels in these legends will stand side by side with the heroes of classical mythology.

Hans Baumann's collection is a welcome and refreshing contribution to worldwide folklore.

Also by Hans Baumann

The Caves of the Great Hunters
In the Land of Ur
The World of the Pharaohs
Lion Gate and Labyrinth
Gold and Gods of Peru
Fenny the Desert Fox

THE STOLEN FIRE

Hans Baumann

THE STOLEN FIRE

LEGENDS OF HEROES AND REBELS FROM AROUND THE WORLD

Translated by Stella Humphries

Illustrated by Herbert Holzing

PANTHEON BOOKS

Published in the United States by Pantheon Books, a division of Random House, Inc., and simultaneously in Canada by Random House of Canada Limited, Toronto.
Originally published in Germany as *Das geraubte Feuer* by Arena-Verlag Georg Popp.

Library of Congress Cataloging in Publication Data

Baumann, Hans, 1914–
The stolen fire.
SUMMARY: A collection of tales from the folklore of Africa, India, China, Australia, North America, Mexico, Russia, and Polynesia.
Translation of Das geraubte Feuer.
1. Tales. [1. Folklore] I. Title.
PZ8.1.B32St 398.2 73-15107
ISBN 0-394-82675-2
ISBN 0-394-92675-7 (lib. bdg.)

Manufactured in the United States of America

Contents

EASTERN EUROPE AND SIBERIA

AFRICA

ASIA AND AUSTRALIA

AMERICA

THE STOLEN FIRE

Introduction

This book contains stories that time has hardly affected. Some are more than five thousand years old, yet they have lost nothing of their impact. This is astonishing, but it is also understandable. These legends are about heroes who fight dragons, resist the oppressor and conquer fear—adventures where everyone must prove himself in his own way.

The present volume is a collection of such legends from all over the world. They come from Africa and India, China and Australia, North America and Mexico, Russia and Polynesia. They tell of Sumerian, Indian, Kara-Kirghiz, Tibetan, Ainu and Pygmy heroes, not forgetting the heroines of the various continents. Just as Siegfried and Theseus kill terrifying monsters, so do Mbega and Onkoito, Kara Khan's daughter and Nana Miriam. They have the courage to defy authority, which always opposes change. Young readers will admire these rebels, whatever their color or their origin. Very often young people understand heroes and dragons much better than their fathers, many of whom deem it wiser to come to terms with dragons.

EASTERN EUROPE AND SIBERIA

Russia

STAVER AND VASSILISSA

Grand Duke Vladimir of Kiev sat banqueting in the great hall of his castle with his princes and boyars around him. Everyone was merry and the feast was already in full swing when it occurred to Vladimir that one of the boyars was not present, the young hero Staver Godinovitch. Immediately the Grand Duke sent a messenger to summon Staver to the merrymaking.

Presently Staver the boyar arrived on horseback. He dismounted and strode through the white stone palace, crossed himself, as was the custom, and bowed to left and right to greet those present. Everyone rose to receive him, even the Grand Duke himself, and Staver saluted him with particular warmth. Then they all sat down again at the oaken tables and the banquet continued.

When the heroes had eaten and drunk their fill, they began to boast, and the loudest of the braggarts were the Grand Duke's men. Nowhere, they insisted, was there more gold, nowhere more silver, nowhere greater heaps of pearls than in the palace of Kiev.

This was too much for Staver. "Listen to those boasters," he murmured in his neighbor's ear. "Their mouths are big, but their heads are empty. They talk and talk of their city of Kiev, its gold, silver and pearls. But what is this stone box compared with my castle? Why, mine is so vast that it's better to ride through it on horseback rather than walk. All the rooms are oak-paneled and hung with beaver and sable. The steel door handles and hinges are all gilded and the floors are made of pure silver. I have iron-bound coffers filled with silver and gold, to say nothing of pearls. And I have a treasure in my house that puts everything else in the shade—my wife, Vassilissa. There is no one to compare with her. Her face is as fair as the freshly fallen snow. She has brows of sable and a falcon's eyes. And she is not only a superb housekeeper, she also knows how to bend the bow and she excels in other manly arts. That's my wife Vassilissa for you!"

Staver had spoken to no one but his neighbor, yet many ears pricked up as he uttered these words. And at once, tale-bearers brought the Grand Duke's notice to the way that Staver had boasted to his fellow guest.

Vladimir flushed with anger. In a voice loud enough for all to hear he said, "Princes and boyars, do you consider it right that someone humiliates me here in my own hall? This Staver Godinovitch is a windbag who insults me with his talk. Seize him and carry him down to the dungeons. Put him behind iron doors and wall up the cell with yellow sand so that he can no longer offend my ears. Then ten of you ride to Staver's castle, seal it up, together with his treasure chests, and bring me the peerless Vassilissa! Bring her here to me, the Grand Duke Vladimir of Kiev!"

Staver was seized and thrown into prison. He was locked behind iron doors and yellow sand, while ten boyars rode off to seal up Staver's castle and to bring Vassilissa to Kiev.

But there was one boyar who was loyal to Staver and he galloped ahead of the others to tell Vassilissa what Vladimir had done to her husband Staver.

Then Vassilissa dressed herself in men's clothing and arranged her hair like a man's. She put on boots of green morocco leather and she armed herself with a goodly sword, a Tartar spear, a bow and a quiver that contained many arrows, all of which she had sharpened with her own hands. So Vassilissa became Vassili. She climbed into her Circassian saddle and with twelve of her men she set out for Kiev.

Halfway there, she met Vladimir's envoys who had been ordered to take Vassilissa prisoner. They did not recognize her and one of them asked her, "Where have you come from, young man, and where are you riding?"

"We have come from the Khan of the Golden Hordes," Vassilissa answered, "to remind the Grand Duke Vladimir that he owes the Khan tribute for the last twelve years. We have orders to take many golden rings back to the Khan, two thousand for each year that is outstanding. And where are you riding?"

At this, the Grand Duke's messengers felt afraid, but at last their leader said, "We are going to Staver's castle, to seal it up and to carry his wife Vassilissa to the Grand Duke Vladimir."

"We have just passed Staver's castle. Vassilissa is not there. She has ridden away."

So Vladimir's envoys returned to Kiev at a gallop to report to the Grand Duke. The latter listened to them with bad grace, and his young wife Apraksiya, too, was greatly out of humor. And when Vassilissa and her attendants came riding up, everyone took her for the ambassador sent by the Khan of the Golden Hordes. The Grand Duke conducted her into the great hall and there he offered her hospitality.

Apraksiya, however, had scrutinized the new arrivals very closely. She led Vladimir away and beneath the portico she said to him softly, "Listen to me, Vladimir. These are no envoys from the Golden Hordes, they have not been sent by the Tartar Khan. Their leader is not a man but Staver's young wife. She sails across the courtyard as a duck swims, and when she sits down, she keeps her knees together."

At this, the Grand Duke recovered his high spirits. He invited all the nobles to a banquet and the merrymaking grew louder than ever. Vassilissa and her attendants were also among the guests. When they had feasted enough, Vladimir said secretly to Apraksiya, "Now I shall put to the test this young man whom the Tartar Khan has sent to me. He shall measure himself at wrestling against my finest champions."

At the table sat seven famous champions: Ilya Murometz, Alyosha Popovitch, Kungur and Suchan, Samson, and Chapil's two sons. No less than five other heroes were also present. The champions challenged Vassilissa to single combat and she declared herself ready to wrestle with them all. They went out into the courtyard, where they lined up in a row.

The first man stepped forth and Vassilissa hit him on the head so hard that he had to be carried from the courtyard. The second had seven of his ribs broken by a single blow of her fist. The third had three of his vertebrae dislocated, and had to crawl away on his hands and knees. The rest took to their heels, not wishing to suffer a similar fate.

Vladimir spat, so great was his rage. When he was alone again with Apraksiya, he said to her, "Your hair may be long, but you haven't much brain. And you say the Khan's envoy is not a man! Why, my court has never seen a hero with such strength."

"Look at her properly," retorted Apraksiya. "Isn't her face as white as freshly fallen snow? Are not her brows like sable? Has she not the bright eyes of the falcon, just as Staver boasted? She is Vassilissa I tell you. You are all blind."

"Very well," said Vladimir. "I shall submit this ambassador to another trial. He shall show us if he can shoot arrows better than my champions."

In an open meadow outside the palace, Vladimir's heroes shot their arrows at an oak tree. Each time it was hit, the oak swayed as if it had been caught in a gust of wind. But when Vassilissa shot her arrow, the bowstring sang, and the mighty oak was felled to the ground, shattered into fragments no bigger than knife handles.

The heroes were dumbfounded.

Vladimir spat for the second time, and he shouted resentfully to Apraksiya, "Look at that oak tree now! I'm not sorry for the tree but for the arrow! We've never seen such an archer here before, and you still believe it's a woman! Now I shall challenge the envoy myself and see if he is also supreme at chess."

He sat down with Vassilissa at an oak chess table and they played with chessmen carved from maplewood. Vassilissa won the first game, then the second and also the third. She laughed, for Vladimir had played for high stakes. Then she pushed the chessboard aside and said to the Grand Duke, "Now let's get down to business. I did not come here to feast with you, nor yet to while away the time playing chess. And the duels with your champions bore me to death. What about the tribute you owe? You have not paid it for twelve whole years. I demand two thousand gold rings for every year. Produce them here and now! The Khan of the Golden Hordes refuses to wait any longer."

Then Vladimir began to whine. "Times are bad you

know. Few merchants still come to Kiev to trade, and there is little collected in taxes. Even fur trapping brings no profit these days. How can I pay?" Then he winked an eye slyly and said in jest, "Why don't you take me and Apraksiya instead of the tribute?"

"What use are you to the Khan of the Golden Hordes? If you have no golden rings, I must take him something that will give him pleasure."

"But what would please him?" asked Vladimir.

"Have you no one who plays the gusla?"

"Yes, indeed. I have the finest gusla player in the land," said Vladimir promptly, for he suddenly remembered that Staver was a most accomplished gusla player. "He is Staver, the young boyar, and he plays the gusla better than anyone else. You may take him as a present to the Tartar Khan."

Vladimir had the yellow sand shoveled away, the iron doors of the dungeon were opened and Staver was led into the great hall. The Grand Duke handed him a gusla and placed him opposite Vassilissa, saying, "Now play for the Khan's ambassador, and then you can return with him to the Golden Hordes. I hope that that will please you."

Staver said nothing but started to play at once. First he played the Great Song of Tsargrad, then he played all the dances and the other pieces that he knew, until Vassilissa said, "He is a good player and I like him better than any tribute, and better than you and your Grand Duchess Apraksiya. I'll take him with me."

Then Vladimir's cares fell from him, and as Vassilissa

and Staver rode away together with their attendants, the Grand Duke cried out joyfully, "The Khan of the Golden Hordes is welcome to that fellow Staver! My gold rings are saved. Come, my heroes! We have good reason to celebrate!"

Russia

DOBRINYA AT THE SARACENS' MOUNT

To Dobrinya, Nikita's son, his mother said, "Oh my Dobrinya, why must you ride to the Saracens' Mount to kill the dragon and free the Russians imprisoned there? No one who has tried to swim the Puchei River has ever returned. It is a fierce beast of prey, with fire leaping from its first rapids, a shower of sparks from the second, and columns of smoke rising from the third."

But Dobrinya, Nikita's son, did not listen to his mother. He rode out to the Saracens' Mount to destroy the dragon's brood and to free the Russian prisoners. And he bathed in the Puchei River and called out, laughing, "Where are your flames, your showers of sparks and your columns of smoke? Why you're nothing but a puddle of rainwater, never a fierce beast of prey!"

Then fire leaped from the first rapids, sparks flew from the second, and the third belched smoke. On the opposite bank, the ferocious dragon with its twelve fangs came out from its lair and said to Dobrinya, "Now tell me, Nikita's son, what shall I do to you? Shall I devour you, or shall I drag you into my cave to join the other Russian prisoners?"

"Accursed dragon!" Dobrinya replied. "You'd like to get me in your clutches and boast about it, wouldn't you? But you haven't got me yet!"

So saying, Dobrinya dived into the Puchei River and swam across it. He surfaced close to the opposite bank on which the dragon stood. But he had neither horse nor lance with him, and as the dragon advanced towards him, he took off his heavy Greek helmet and smote the dragon with such force that six of its fangs were torn off. Dobrinya forced the monster to the ground with his knees and took out his dagger to stab it.

"Let me live a little longer," the dragon implored him, "and I shall obey you as a child obeys his big brother. And I promise never to fly to Russia again in order to snatch my prey."

So Dobrinya made a pact with the dragon. He stood up and allowed it to rise. Then it flew away into the steppes.

The following year, Dobrinya went to Kiev to visit the Grand Duke Vladimir, and the Grand Duke said to him, "We are in deep mourning. The accursed dragon has flown over the city and has seized my niece Sabava." He spoke these words to Dobrinya and to another hero, Alyosha, who was also present, and he asked them, "Which of you will bring her back? Who is willing to fight the dragon?"

"Why need there be a fight at all?" asked Alyosha.

"Dobrinya has made a pact with the dragon. If Dobrinya demands it, the monster is obliged to release Sabava."

"If that is so, go and fetch her, Dobrinya," said Vladimir. "Or else I shall have your head chopped off, you dragon's brother!"

Dobrinya did not know what to do and so he went to his mother. When she saw him coming, she asked him, "What is wrong, Dobrinya? Has some fool mocked you, or did a drunkard laugh at you?"

"Not a fool, nor yet a drunkard," said Dobrinya. "The Grand Duke Vladimir has me in a cleft stick. Either I must free his niece from the dragon's cave, or else he will have my head chopped off."

No sooner had she heard this than Dobrinya's mother fetched Nikita's fine chestnut horse from its stable and fed it with maize. Dobrinya threw three felt blankets over its back and on top of them he placed a Circassian saddle. His mother handed him a silken whip, saying, "Now ride away to the Saracens' Mount, trample the dragon's brood to death, and rescue the Russian prisoners from its cave. And if the chestnut shies when the dragon's young throng around its hoofs, then lash its legs with this silken whip."

So Dobrinya took his leave more swiftly than the east wind. One saw him as he leaped into the saddle, but the next moment he had gone. When he arrived at the Saracens' Mount, he tried to trample the dragon's whelps, but they clustered around the horse's fetlocks and the chestnut was terrified. Then Dobrinya lashed it with his silken whip and so he was able to ride on towards the dragon's lair to free the Russian captives.

The dragon darted out from the farthest corner of its cave and confronted Dobrinya. "Big brother!" it roared. "Why do you break our pact?"

"Come here, you accursed reptile!" replied Dobrinya. "Come here you breaker of promises! Where have you hidden Vladimir's niece? Give me Sabava at once, without fighting or bloodshed!"

The dragon refused and a great battle began. For three days Dobrinya fought with the dragon, but he could not subdue the fiendish monster.

At last his strength was exhausted and he was about to admit defeat, when he heard his mother's voice calling him, "Crush the dragon's brood and rescue Sabava from the monster's cave!"

So Dobrinya fought on for another three hours and at last he killed the dragon. East and west its blood flowed down the sides of the mountain. Dobrinya mounted his horse, ready to gallop away, when he heard his mother's voice once more, "Stay where you are and strike the wet earth with your lance! Pound it with your lance until the earth opens and swallows the accursed dragon's brood!"

Dobrinya obeyed and struck the ground with his lance. The earth opened and swallowed the dragon's whelps. So Dobrinya jumped down from his fine horse and explored the winding paths within the dragon's lair. Then he led the Russian prisoners outside, peasants, nobles and sons of princes; and from the deepest recess of all, he freed Sabava and led her forth into the bright light of day.

Next he addressed the Russians whom he had wrested from the dragon, and to the peasants, nobles and sons of princes he said, "Go home, all of you—go to those who are waiting for you. You need not be afraid of the dragon now. The monster is dead, slain by Dobrinya, Nikita's son. No one need fear it any longer."

Then all the Russians thanked him. But Dobrinya lifted Sabava onto the saddle before him, and took her back to Grand Duke Vladimir of Kiev. Then he rode home to his mother.

Caucasus

URISMAG

Urismag, the great hero of the Nart tribe, realized one day that he had grown old. The others had noticed this some time before, and they no longer expected him to perform great deeds. The young men had stopped asking him for advice, and the older men, who had already made a name for themselves, treated him with contempt. Many even went so far as to laugh at Urismag. The aged hero passed his time watching the others at archery. He walked about as if he were in a daze.

One day, he was sitting in the great square where the men used to meet. After he had listened for a while to the way they conversed among themselves, he said, "I know that I have become a burden to you."

The men contradicted him, and one of the elders declared, "No one else has performed such deeds, none has ever given us wiser counsel."

"But now I am good for nothing. My brain is worn out.

The best thing you can do is to make me a coffin, place me in it and throw me into the river that flows down to the Black Sea. Then you will be rid of me."

The Narts protested, but Urismag said, "For fifty years you have obeyed me. For the last time, I insist that you do as I wish."

And so they obeyed him. They made a big coffin and Urismag lay down inside it. They gave him plenty of food, and once more the aged hero's face wore the cheerful expression that his subjects knew so well. "Now I shall make the journey that I have dreamed of all my life," said Urismag as they closed the coffin.

For six days and seven nights the river carried him. In the course of the seventh night, the coffin was washed ashore at a place where horses were watered. These horses belonged to the Lord of the Black Sea, the deadly enemy of the Narts.

When the horses came down to drink at daybreak, they saw the coffin and scattered in all directions, whinnying with fear. The herdsmen put their heads together and then decided to open the big box. When they saw the old man lying in the coffin, they were flabbergasted. The old man laughed and said, "Good morning!"

"Who are you? Where have you come from?" asked the herdsmen.

"I come from the Land of the Narts," said Urismag, and he told them his name.

Then the men scattered in panic exactly as the horses

had done, and one of them rushed into the castle of the Lord of the Black Sea and said, "Even if you kill me for it, I must tell you: the man you have hunted with such hatred for so many years has fallen into your hands. He is the Nart chieftain, Urismag. He came floating down the river in a coffin, and the waters washed it up on the bank where your horses go down to drink."

"Bring him here at once!" ordered the Lord of the Black Sea.

When the herdsmen returned with Urismag, the Lord of the Black Sea rejoiced as never before in his life. He had the old man clapped in irons, to which were attached heavy logs of wood to weigh down his legs. He was thrown into the dungeon of a tower and given nothing but bread and water.

One day, he spoke to the man who brought him his bread. "Your master is a fool," he declared. "What good does it do him if I rot away my life here in this dungeon? My death will bring him no reward. Instead, he could get a huge ransom for me. After all, I am an old man whom he need no longer fear."

The guard went to the Lord of the Black Sea and said to him, "Even if you kill me for it, I must tell you: Urismag has called you a fool. In his opinion, you could get a handsome ransom for him. After all, he is an old man, whom you need no longer fear."

Then the Lord of the Black Sea had Urismag fetched from the dungeon and said to him, "What is this nonsense about a ransom? What are you after all but a miserable cur?"

"You are quite wrong," said Urismag. "The Narts will ransom me for three times the fortune that I possess."

"And how much is that?"

"Listen to my offer," said Urismag, "and then tell me if it will be enough. I offer you the following—

Ten thousand cattle each with one horn
Ten thousand cattle each with two horns
Ten thousand cattle each with three horns
Ten thousand cattle each with four horns
Ten thousand cattle each with five horns.

"In that case, I agree," said the Lord of the Black Sea. "I shall send messengers to the Narts immediately."

"Good," said Urismag. "Send one dark-haired man and one with fair hair."

"As you wish," said the Lord of the Black Sea.

Then Urismag gave the two messengers the following commission, "Tell the Narts that I am a prisoner here and that they must send a herd of cattle for my ransom—

Ten thousand cattle each with one horn
Ten thousand cattle each with two horns
Ten thousand cattle each with three horns
Ten thousand cattle each with four horns
Ten thousand cattle each with five horns.

"A black ox and a yellow one shall lead the herd. And if

these leaders should try to go astray, the Narts must cut off the head of the black ox and hang it around the yellow one's neck. Then the yellow ox will keep to the right path."

The two messengers journeyed to the Land of the Narts and they found the men assembled in the great square. "We wish you joy," they said.

"Where have you come from and who are you?" asked the Narts. "What brings you here?"

"We have come to end your sorrow," said the messengers. "We have been sent by Urismag. He has fallen into the hands of the Lord of the Black Sea."

"That only increases our sorrow," said the Narts.

"Urismag will be set free if you pay a ransom for him," the messengers continued.

At this the Narts rejoiced and asked, "How much?"

The messengers repeated word for word what Urismag had told them to say. The Narts must send five times ten thousand head of cattle.

Ten thousand cattle each with one horn
Ten thousand cattle each with two horns
Ten thousand cattle each with three horns
Ten thousand cattle each with four horns
Ten thousand cattle each with five horns.

They added that the herd must be led by a black and a yellow ox, and that they should behead the black one if it strayed from the right path.

The Narts listened in tense silence. At last, one of them

spoke, "One-horned cattle are easy to find. We need only cut off one of their horns. And two-horned oxen we have in plenty. But where shall we find oxen with three, four or five horns?"

"Let us go to Urismag's wife, Satana," said another. "She is the wisest of women. Satana knows everything."

So three men were sent to Satana and they repeated word for word what the messengers had said, not forgetting the order to cut off the black ox's head and hang it around the neck of the yellow ox should these two try to mislead the herd.

"What a cunning fellow Urismag is!" laughed Satana. "Don't you understand his message? He has set you a riddle and here is the answer to it:

A one-horned ox is a soldier with a battle-axe
A two-horned ox is a soldier with sword and spear
A three-horned ox is a soldier with three weapons
A four-horned ox is a horseman without armor
A five-horned ox is a horseman fully armed.

"And the leading oxen are the two messengers from the Lord of the Black Sea, one dark and the other fair. Should they try to lead our army astray, you need only cut off the head of one of them, and then the other will be sure to guide you safely to the place where Urismag is waiting for you. Now hurry and do as your chieftain says. The old man is more than a match for you still."

The three Narts hurried to tell the others. For three days

they feasted the messengers. And for three days they armed themselves, preparing for the march. They put the messengers at the head of the army and when they tried to lead the Narts the wrong way, they chopped off the head of the dark-haired messenger and hung it around the neck of the fair-haired one. Then the latter led the army by the shortest route into the Land of the Lord of the Black Sea.

Meanwhile, Urismag had worked out how soon he could expect the messengers' return, together with the Nart army. And when the time had come, he said to the Lord of the Black Sea, "Let us go to the top of the tower and see if my ransom is coming, the herd with five times ten thousand cattle."

They climbed to the top of the tower and in the distance they saw a dark mass surging towards them across the plains. Then Urismag said, "Send out all your men to meet them right away. And let each one take a stick with him. Such a great herd needs many men to drive it."

The Lord of the Black Sea was so greedy for the cattle that he immediately sent out his men with sticks. But when they clashed with the well-armed warriors from the Land of the Narts, the Lord of the Black Sea's men were all killed. A great cloud of dust arose from the tumult.

"What does this mean?" asked the Lord of the Black Sea.

"It is the dust churned up by so many hoofs, with the steam from so many nostrils," replied Urismag.

"It sounds more like the clang of arms," said the Lord of the Black Sea.

"It is the clashing of so many horns," said Urismag, "the stamping of so many hoofs."

"You are lying!" shouted the Lord of the Black Sea.

Then Urismag struck him across the face, saying, "Ever since I have known you, Lord of the Black Sea, you have wanted to kill me!" And he gave him a hard push, so that the Lord of the Black Sea fell from the top of the tower to his death.

The Nart army marched up and greeted the aged hero Urismag with wild rejoicing.

"What have you to say now?" cried Urismag to his people. "Even an old head is still worth something. The ravens would have picked your bones before any of you would have dared to play such a trick on your deadliest enemy."

Then the Narts returned to their own country, taking with them all the cattle and treasure belonging to the Lord of the Black Sea, and each of the fighting men received his fair share of the booty.

Bulgaria

GEORGE IN THE REALM OF DARKNESS

George the shepherd was a man of few words but he was as strong as a lion. His two brothers envied him on account of his strength. One noontime, they overpowered him as he slept and threw him into a very deep well which had run dry. At the bottom of the well two rams were waiting, one black and the other white. George seized the black ram and it carried him through a long passage into the Realm of Darkness. There all the people were black, including the Tsar. When George appeared before the black Tsar, riding on the black ram, the Tsar asked him, "Are you really as strong as people say?"

"Perhaps," was George's answer.

"And brave with it?"

"It seems so."

"And have you a heart for those in trouble?"

"That I have," said George the shepherd.

"Then you're the man," said the black Tsar.

"The man for what?"

"The man to free my daughter from the dragon who has drunk the well dry, who eats human flesh and who stinks abominably. Will you face this dragon?"

"I will," said George.

So the black Tsar himself led George to the cave where his daughter was held prisoner by the dragon. The Tsar remained at a safe distance, but George stepped up to the cave's entrance from which emerged a cloud of foul smoke.

"Come out, you skunk!" cried George, in such a loud voice that the cave wall cracked.

The furious dragon started from its cave and opened its huge mouth. But George aimed such a powerful kick inside the monster's jaws that its skull was completely shattered.

"Is it dead?" called the Tsar from the distance.

"As a stone," answered George.

At this, the black Tsar came running up, but George went inside the cave and brought out the Tsar's daughter, who was also black. The Tsar wanted her to be George's wife. "When I am dead and gone, you shall be Tsar in the Realm of Darkness. You'd like that, wouldn't you?"

"I can't."

"Why not?" asked the Tsar, and his looks grew blacker than ever.

"Because I have something important to do in the Realm of Light."

"Is there anything more important than marrying the Tsar's daughter and becoming Tsar yourself?"

"Yes, there is," said George. "My brothers threw me into the empty well, and I must settle my score with them."

The black Tsar had to agree to this and he allowed George to go.

George returned through the long passage down which the black ram had carried him, and when he reached the bottom of the well, he found the white ram and sat on its back. Immediately the white ram began to run, and it carried George back to the Realm of Light. George thanked the white ram and returned to his brothers. The latter shrank in terror when they saw him coming. But George ordered them to go with him to fell trees in the forest. The brothers followed him meekly.

Inside the forest, George raised his big axe and stretched himself to his full height. With a single powerful stroke, he split a beech tree from crown to base in such a way that the two halves remained touching each other. Then with his hands, George held the halves apart and told his brothers to help him separate them. The brothers obeyed and placed their hands inside the cleft. George quickly jumped away, letting the two halves go. They sprang together and trapped the brothers' hands, so that they were completely flattened out. For a day and a night George left his brothers trapped helplessly in the beech tree. Then he released them.

And since that time, so they say, human beings have had hands with palms, and fingers that can move. Before, they only had fists which they could not open.

South Siberia

TARDANAK

Tardanak was working in his field when up came the seven-headed Yelbeggen, carrying a big sack which he opened. The monster bared the fangs of six of his heads and with the seventh he said, "Come along, Tardanak, jump into my sack."

Tardanak had no weapon with which to defend himself, so he did not try to resist. The Yelbeggen dropped him in the sack, threw it over his shoulder and set off for home. As he walked, however, he grew tired and sat down to rest. Soon he fell asleep and began snoring most horribly. Tardanak crawled out and tore up bushes and plants with which he filled the sack. Then he returned home and went on with his farming.

After three hours, the Yelbeggen awoke, but he still felt sleepy. He carried the sack home and the Yelbeggen children rushed up to see what there was inside the sack.

"Father has brought us bushes and plants to play with!" cried the little monsters, who all had seven heads like their father.

"There are no bushes in my sack," protested the Yelbeggen with all his seven heads. "What I have in my sack is Tardanak."

The children did not answer and the terrible Yelbeggen looked inside the sack for himself. He pulled out all the plants and bushes, but there was no sign of Tardanak.

So the seven-headed Yelbeggen went back again and found Tardanak at work in his field once more.

"Well, Tardanak," said the Yelbeggen, "Wouldn't you like to jump in my sack once more?"

"Why not?" answered Tardanak, for he knew there was no escape.

The Yelbeggen seized him and dropped him into the big sack. But this time the monster did not rest by the wayside. He carried the sack straight home and hung it securely from the ceiling.

"What kind of wood will you use to cook me?" asked Tardanak from inside the sack.

"Pine twigs," said the Yelbeggen, and he went into the wood to fetch some.

While he was away, the Yelbeggen's children came closer to the sack and asked, "Tardanak, are you inside there?"

"I am," replied Tardanak. "Don't you want to play with me?"

"We'd like to, but we're not allowed," they answered.

"Very well then, don't play with me," said Tardanak. "But I could make you some arrows and feather them for you."

Immediately the little monsters untied the big sack and Tardanak at once cut off their seven heads and threw the bodies into the cauldron that had been intended for him. Then he dug a hole beside the hearth and when it was finished, he hid himself in a corner.

The Yelbeggen came home and immediately glanced in the cauldron. "Very good!" he said. "I see that Tardanak is already dead and cooked. Come on children," he called with all his seven heads. "Let's have Tardanak for dinner."

The children did not come.

"Children, where are you?" cried the Yelbeggen once more.

But still they did not appear. Then the Yelbeggen went over to the bench, and when he pulled it out, the monsters' heads rolled towards him.

Then he realized that Tardanak had outwitted his brood and that he must be still alive.

"Where are you, Tardanak?" the seven heads called.

"Here outside. I'm fetching wood."

The Yelbeggen went outside, but there was no Tardanak to be seen. "Where are you Tardanak?" he repeated, shouting louder than ever.

"I'm here indoors," called Tardanak. "I'm putting more wood on the fire."

The Yelbeggen dashed back into the house, but there was no sign of Tardanak.

By now, the monster was seething with rage. He darted outside again, ran around the house, then back inside again, looking everywhere. At last he noticed the hole beside the hearth.

"Are you in the hole, Tardanak?" asked the Yelbeggen's seven heads.

There was no answer.

"You're in there, I know you are!" the monster shouted. "You can't be anywhere else." And he stuck all his seven heads inside the hole, burrowing his way deeper and deeper until he was stuck as surely as a hitching post that has been firmly rammed home.

"Here I am!" shouted Tardanak. He leaped from his hiding place, and poured the boiling mixture from the cauldron all over the Yelbeggen. And so the monster was dead.

Then Tardanak returned home, and went on plowing his field.

KARA KHAN'S DAUGHTER

Kara Khan rode only black horses, ruled over many people and had large herds of cattle. But his only child was a daughter named Altyn Aryg, and the fact that he had no son caused him deep concern.

"My strength is waning and I have no son," he grieved as he rode away to see that justice was done among his people and that his herds were well cared for. When he returned home, he was exhausted after the long journey, for it took him a long time to cover all the territory he governed. "Many are my people and many are my cattle. It is all too much for me," he said to his daughter. "I wish that my father beneath the earth would gather to himself half my people and half my herds."

"But before that could happen," replied Altyn Aryg, "half your people and half your cattle would have to be buried in the ground."

"It would be better so," said Kara Khan.

Then Altyn Aryg grew angry and said to her father, "How can you wish for such a thing, just because you are old! It would be better to hand over your people and your livestock to me, so that I can care for them, since you have no son."

"That is no task for a girl," said Kara Khan firmly.

"I can do it," insisted Altyn Aryg. "The time has come for you to bequeath to me your people and your cattle."

"How dare you speak like that!" cried Kara Khan. "I shall never hand over my subjects and my herds to a girl."

"Then I shall leave you," said Altyn Aryg. "We'll soon see whether or not a girl can do the things that a father usually entrusts to his sons."

So Altyn Aryg departed from her father's tent. She rode away and presently she came to another tent and said, "I am Kara Khan's daughter, Altyn Aryg."

This tent belonged to Altyn Khan, who was famous for his brave deeds. "Where are you going and what do you seek?" he asked Altyn Aryg. "How does it happen that a girl rides alone and forsakes her father's tent?"

"I have left my father's tent because he will not hand over to me the care of his people and his cattle," said Altyn Aryg. "I am on my way to find the Snake Prince, who devours human flesh."

When Altyn Khan heard this, he trembled, for the Snake Prince had eaten so many people that no one dared to fight him. Everyone paid him tribute, even renowned heroes, and everyone was frightened of the monster's cunning.

"Go home," said Altyn Khan. "He will eat you too if you go too close."

"I shall kill the Snake Prince," said the girl.

The next day, Altyn Aryg journeyed on. And after seven days she came to the Snake Prince. He was so terrifying that no bird remained in the air in his presence. The wild beasts stood spellbound unable to move away.

The Snake Prince was enormous, his mouth was huge. One lip brushed the sky, the other grazed the ground. His brow touched the sky, his chin rested on the ground. This great mouth had swallowed many heroes, not to mention birds and beasts. They were imprisoned inside the Snake Prince, whose body was like a vast cavern.

The girl stepped inside the gigantic jaws and entered the great cavern. She peered at the monster's heart and touched it. The heart was huge and as hard as rock. "How can one kill this heart?" Altyn Aryg asked the heroes.

"One cannot kill it," they replied. "We have tried. You will find that no one can pierce the monster's heart."

The heroes gave Altyn Aryg their swords and she tried them one after the other. And since she struck with greater strength than any of the others, their swords were all shattered, but the heart itself remained unhurt.

So Altyn Aryg drew her own sword and with it she inflicted such a deep wound that the Snake Prince gasped and opened his mouth in terror. The open mouth remained, even after he was dead.

"You have saved us," said the heroes to the girl as they

walked out into the open air. They offered to pay her the tribute that the Snake Prince had exacted from them.

But Altyn Aryg refused. "I want no tribute from anyone. I set out to kill the monster who oppressed others and held them prisoner. You heroes shall live as you used to, before the Snake Prince forced you to do his will."

"Will you return home empty handed?" asked one of them in amazement.

The girl laughed. "Now I have things to tell my father. And when he has heard me, I do not think that my hands will remain empty."

Altyn Aryg went back home and her father rejoiced to see her once more in his tent. Her mother hastened to prepare a great feast, to which all their neighbors were invited.

"Where have you come from, my child?" asked Kara Khan.

"From a cave, from a gateway as high as the sky," answered Altyn Aryg. "The gateway was the great mouth of the Snake Prince. The cave was his belly, in which he kept many heroes imprisoned and also beasts and birds. But when I pierced his enormous heart with your sword, the Snake Prince died. And all the birds, beasts and heroes inside its body could go free."

When they heard this, everyone was astounded and Kara Khan said, "You are strong, my daughter. That is good. I shall hand over to you my people and my cattle. Now I can die in peace."

And so Altyn Aryg inherited her father's people and his cattle together with his tent.

When Kara Khan died, there was a great banquet in his honor but the girl said, "Now there is no man in the tent. It is not good to live without a man."

Time went by and a man rode up to Atlyn Aryg's tent and asked her, "Will you not marry me? My name is Katkanjyla, and all I own is my horse."

Then Altyn Aryg married him. Her tent became his and he cared for her subjects and the herds that belonged to the tent. The people accepted him, and the cattle, too, were better off afterwards.

Estonia

THE HERALD OF WAR

The King of Estonia made up his mind to go to war again. He summoned his four heralds and gave them his secret orders. These were, that in twelve days' time, all able-bodied men must assemble fully armed for an attack upon Finland.

The king told the four heralds, "You ride to the west, you to the east, you to the south, and you to the north, to the Finnish Bridge. Everything depends on these secret orders being delivered swiftly and without fail. Only if we make a surprise attack in full strength can we defeat the Finns."

The couriers sprang onto their horses and each rode off in the direction he had been given. The western herald, the eastern herald, and the southern herald rode obediently from farm to farm, showing the secret call to arms to every man they met. And the people armed themselves, in readiness for war.

On the second day, the northern herald, he whose destination was the Finnish Bridge, was suddenly intercepted. A bedraggled old crow alighted on the road before him, just as his horse approached.

"Wait, wait!" croaked the crow.

"I have no time," replied the herald.

"Is it war? Is it war?" asked the crow hoarsely.

"What nonsense!" answered the herald.

"You smell of blood, of many dead," croaked the crow. "You and I go hand in hand."

The herald spurred on his horse, but the crow followed him. Then the herald thought, "The crow is right. There will be many dead."

A little later, a vulture barred his way and addressed him in these words, "You smell of blood, of many dead."

"Out of my way!" ordered the herald.

"You need only tell me where we are to meet," said the vulture. "I am invited too."

"Make way there!" shouted the herald and galloped on. But the vulture followed him.

"What it says is true," the herald reflected. "Wherever swords and spears do their duty, wherever arrows and battle-axes bite deep into human flesh, a banquet is spread for birds of carrion."

Then a wolf appeared at the roadside. "You smell of blood, of many dead," said the wolf. "Have you an invitation for me in your pocket? You and I go hand in hand."

The herald made no reply. He spurred on his horse, but

the wolf loped after him and again the man thought, "The wolf is right. The secret orders I must deliver will cost many men their lives."

Suddenly the horse shied at a dark figure crouching beside the road.

"What do you want? Who are you?" demanded the herald.

"I am Famine," said the figure, straightening her back until she towered above the horse. "Haven't you a letter for me as well? You smell of blood, of many dead. Wherever there is war, I belong on the scene. When men are slain with sword and battle-axe, then women and children die too. When fields of grain are trampled and barns are set on fire, many must die of hunger."

The herald rode past the figure in silence. But when he turned his head, he was appalled to see that she was following him with giant strides.

By now, the herald was close to the Finnish Bridge and then he was stopped for the fifth time. A hideous old hag shuffled towards him saying, "I am Pestilence. I too belong on the scene. I shall account for more dead than ever those slain by the men to whom you carry your secret orders. I am the mightiest of those in your wake."

"Ride on!" said Famine. "We all belong on the scene, wherever war is waged. Your secret orders are addressed to all of us as well."

At that, the herald was seized with horror. He swung around abandoning the road that led to the Finnish Bridge.

He rode no longer from farm to farm, mustering the men. He galloped full tilt until he reached the coast. There he reined in his horse, tore the secret orders from his coat and flung them into the sea.

Shoals of fish were swimming past. But when they collided with the secret orders, they scattered in all directions, fleeing away in panic.

The train of followers fell upon the messenger.

"You have cheated us!" Famine reproached him.

The birds of prey attacked him viciously. But the herald warded them off and rode on until he reached another country. The king waited in vain for him and a quarter of the army he needed.

"You are a traitor!" shrieked Pestilence.

And so there was no war.

AFRICA

East Africa

BIG KIHUO AND LITTLE KIHUO

A long time ago, the Vakishamba tribe had a chief whose ambition it was to remain chief for as long as possible. So he did not mind when year after year only daughters were born to his wife. But one day a son came into the world. The chief called him Kihuo and he feared him from the start. However, during the child's early years, his father's fear did not increase, for Kihuo grew but slowly and remained very small.

The chief mocked him for his size, even in front of strangers. And when Kihuo grew to manhood, his father would not allow him to enter the community of men. "You must grow properly first," he said to his son. "Little Kihuo must become Big Kihuo. Only then can you undergo the three ordeals."

Kihuo tried to protest, but his father refused to listen to him. So secretly, Kihuo left the tribal territory and went to a chief who would listen to him.

Kihuo said, "I have begged my father to submit me to the three ordeals and to declare me a man. But he refuses and says that I am too small. However, I have prepared myself for the tests in secret. I have practiced throwing the club, my right arm has grown strong with exercise, and my throws are sure."

"Let us try you out then," said the other chief.

They went into the bush, and when a hyena crossed their path, Kihuo threw his club and the hyena's skull was shattered.

"A throw like that would have killed even a lion," said the chief. "But what about your courage? Are you prepared to creep into a herd of elephants and to sleep in their midst?"

So Kihuo crept in among a herd of elephants, slept there all night and escaped safely.

"You have passed the second test too," said the chief. "How about your cunning?"

Kihuo smiled and said, "Am I not playing a trick on my father here and now? He wanted to keep me as a child, and now I have proved what I can do."

Then the other chief initiated him into manhood and from that day, Kihuo started to grow. He returned to his own tribe, went out hunting with the other men and excelled before all others. When he threw his club, it never failed to hit its target.

Now his father trembled before him. He tried to incite the other warriors of the tribe to oppose Kihuo. But the warriors were loyal to the young man. The old chief became ridiculous in their eyes. One day, they appointed Kihuo as their chief and they gave the old man a stick to carry in his hand, saying, "From today, you will be called Memsenge, the man with the stick. From today, Kihuo is our chief."

The man with the stick grew too weak to bear the mockery of the others and so he went away. Kihuo now grew taller still. Day after day he thought of ways to enlarge his tribe's territory, so as to make the Vakishamba people the most powerful tribe, and he dreamed of becoming the greatest of all chiefs.

The nearest tribe to the north he conquered by a trick. He invited the men to come and, together with his own warriors, he led them to the biggest tree for many miles around. Then he said, "Let us carve vessels from this tree. It has so much wood that there will be enough for both our tribes. We Vakishamba people will do the really hard work, which is the felling. You others need only catch the tree as it falls, to make sure that it does not splinter and thus waste much of the wood."

The Vakishamba men set to work and their axes bit deep into the mighty trunk. When it fell, it descended like a mountain on those below whom Kihuo had invited. Many of them were killed outright. Those who escaped with their lives were overpowered by Kihuo's soldiers. Thus did the Vakishamba double their territory at a single stroke. Now, whenever they spoke of their chief, the warriors called him The Great Kihuo.

But he was not yet satisfied with his success. The people to the west were governed by a chief named Orombo, who was very tall. The tallest of his warriors came only to his chest. He often waged war and had already seized much land from his neighbors. In spite of it all, he was hated by his people. For he found pleasure in oppressing those he should have cared for. Wherever he went, he gave orders.

"Bring stones!" he cried and men and women had to carry stones to the place where Orombo stood. No one knew what he wanted to do with the stones.

"Bring planks!" he ordered, and everyone had to drag huge planks which were never used.

One day, he made his warriors chew wormwood roots for his women. These roots are bitter, their juice makes the mouth and the cheeks swell most painfully. The warriors chewed from morning till night, until none of them could close his mouth for the swelling. A man to whom a child was born that day, called it Kyasama, which means Open Mouth.

Orombo was as strong as a giant. He could lift a barrel of beer which needed four men to carry it, put it to his lips and empty it at a draught. Once, in doing so, he swallowed a lizard that had fallen from a tree. It made him vomit all the beer he had drunk and when he saw the lizard lying before him on the ground, he flew into a rage and commanded his men to kill all the lizards in the land. Thus began a great slaughter of the lizards.

In these ways he tyrannized his tribe, but no one would

dare to rebel against him, although they all despised him.

Kihuo saw that here was an opportunity to increase his own glory, and also to get rid of Orombo. He staked everything on his skill at throwing the club and he challenged Orombo to a duel. All the warriors of both tribes were to witness the contest and to accept the winner as chief. Orombo laughed when he heard the challenge. He emptied a whole barrel of beer and said, "Now I'm going to enjoy myself."

Kihuo took six days to prepare himself for the fight. On the first day he killed a jackal, on the second a buffalo, on the third a leopard, on the fourth a lion, on the fifth an elephant, and on the sixth a vulture.

On the seventh day, the two chiefs met between their massed armies. Orombo swung a great spear and cried, "Where are you, Little Kihuo? Where have you gone, you dwarf?"

He flung his spear, but Kihuo ducked and the spear flew into the earth behind him, as a snake vanishes into its hole.

Next Kihuo threw his club, and before Orombo could say "*Tsa*!" it stuck in his skull. As he fell, it was not only Kihuo's men who shouted for joy. Orombo's warriors too joined in the cries of victory and made Kihuo their chief.

Kihuo now thought about expanding his territory to the south. The neighboring tribe to the south, however, was very large and they relied on their great numbers.

Kihuo pondered for six whole days before he thought of a new strategy. Then he confronted them with an army that had doubled overnight. Kihuo had ordered all the young women of the tribe to disguise themselves as warriors and to march into battle. As soon as the opposing chief saw superior numbers advancing, he ordered a retreat and surrendered half his land to the Vakishamba.

By now, Kihuo had so enlarged his power that he dared to challenge the Moshi, who had never been defeated by any other tribe.

Kihuo took no girls with him on this campaign, for the Moshi chief was not so easy to deceive. He had the eyes of an eagle, the lion's quickness to pick up a scent, and the hearing of the elephant's heart. His warriors were devoted to him. They were ready to defend their land.

These things were known to Kihuo's men and they marched along with drooping heads. In the plains before the Land of the Moshi, Kihuo halted his army. "Separate and gather stones," he said to his men. "Let each of you find a stone and then we shall make a heap of the stones, so that we can see how powerful we are."

This they did. Every soldier picked up a stone and placed it on a heap. So a big hill of stones arose and the warriors called it Big Kihuo. Now they were full of self-confidence and they marched into the Land of the Moshi. But they were thoroughly beaten by the Moshi and they suffered such great losses that they had to retreat at the double.

When they came to the hill of stones that they had piled on the previous day, Kihuo told them to halt. "Let us gather stones again and make them into another heap," he ordered. This they did and everyone could see that it was a pathetic little hillock. From this they knew how many of them had been killed in battle. And Kihuo himself called it Little Kihuo.

From that day on, he never went to war again.

Nigeria

NANA MIRIAM

Fara Maka was a man of the Songai tribe, who lived by the River Niger. He was taller than the other men and he was also stronger. Only he was very ugly. However, no one thought that important, because Fara Maka had a daughter who was very beautiful. Her name was Nana Miriam and she too was tall and strong. Her father instructed her in all kinds of things. He went with her to the sandbank and said, "Watch the fish!" And he told her the names of all the various kinds. Everything there is to know about fish he taught her. Then he asked her, "What kind is the one swimming here, and the other one over there?"

"This is a so-and-so," replied Nana Miriam. "And that is a such-and-such."

"Male or female?" asked Fara Maka.

"I don't know," said Nana Miriam.

"This one is a female, and so is the other one," explained Fara Maka. "But the third one over there is a male." And each time he pointed to a different fish.

That was how Nana Miriam came to learn so much. And in addition she had magic powers within her, which no one suspected. And because her father also taught her many magic spells, she grew stronger than anyone else in the Land of the Songai.

Beside the great river, the Niger, there lived a monster that took the form of a hippopotamus. This monster was insatiable. It broke into the rice fields and devoured the crops, bringing famine to the Songai people. No one could tackle this hippopotamus, because it could change its shape. So the hunters had all their trouble for nothing and they returned to their villages in helpless despair. Times were so bad that many died of hunger.

One day, Fara Maka picked up all his lances and set out to kill the monster. When he saw it, he recoiled in fear, for huge pots of fire were hung around the animal's neck. Fara Maka hurled lance after lance, but each one was swallowed by the flames. The hippopotamus monster looked at Fara Maka with scorn. Then it turned its back on him and trotted away.

Fara Maka returned home furious, wondering who he could summon to help him. Now there was a man of the Tomma tribe who was a great hunter. His name was Kara-Digi-Mao-Fosi-Fasi, and Fara Maka asked him if he would hunt the hippopotamus with his one hundred and twenty dogs. "That I will," said Kara-Digi-Mao-Fosi-Fasi.

So Fara Maka invited him and his one hundred and twenty dogs to a great banquet. Before every dog, which had an iron chain around its neck, was placed a small mound of rice and meat. For the hunter, however, there was a huge mound of rice. None of the dogs left a single grain of rice uneaten, and neither did Kara-Digi-Mao-Fosi-Fasi. Well fortified, they set out for the place where the monster lived.

As soon as the dogs picked up the scent, Kara-Digi-Mao-Fosi-Fasi unchained the first one. The chain rattled as the dog leaped forward towards its quarry. One chain rattled after the other, as dog after dog sprang forward to attack the hippopotamus. But the hippopotamus took them on one by one, and it gobbled them all up. The great hunter Kara-Digi-Mao-Fosi-Fasi took to his heels in terror. The hippopotamus charged into a rice field and ate that too.

When Fara Maka heard from the great hunter what had happened, he sat down in the shadow of a large tree and hung his head.

"Haven't you been able to kill the hippopotamus?" Nana Miriam asked him.

"No," said Fara Maka.

"And Kara-Digi-Mao-Fosi-Fasi couldn't drive it away either?"

"No."

"So there is no one who can get the better of it?"

"No," said Fara Maka.

"Then I'll not delay any longer," said Nana Miriam. "I'll go to its haunts and see what I can see."

"Yes, do," said her father.

Nana Miriam walked along the banks of the Niger, and she soon found the hippopotamus eating its way through a rice field. As soon as it saw the girl it stopped eating, raised its head and greeted her.

"Good morning," replied Nana Miriam.

"I know why you have come," said the hippopotamus. "You want to kill me. But no one can do that. Your father tried, and he lost all his lances. The great hunter Kara-Digi-Mao-Fosi-Fasi tried, and all his dogs paid with their lives for his presumption. And you are only a girl."

"We'll soon see," answered Nana Miriam. "Prepare to fight with me. Only one of us will be left to tell the tale."

"Right you are!" shouted the hippopotamus and with its breath it set the rice field afire. There it stood in a ring of flame through which no mortal could pass.

But Nana Miriam threw magic powder into the fire, and the flames turned to water.

"Right!" shouted the hippopotamus, and a wall of iron sprang up making a ring around the monster. But Nana Miriam plucked a magic hammer from the air, and shattered the iron wall into fragments.

Now for the first time the hippopotamus felt afraid, and it turned itself into a river that flowed into the Niger.

Again Nana Miriam sprinkled her magic powder. At once the river dried up and the water changed back into a hippopotamus. It grew more and more afraid and when Fara Maka came up to see what was happening, the monster charged him blindly. Nana Miriam ran after it, and when it was only ten bounds away from her father, she seized it by its left hind foot and flung it across the Niger. As it crashed against the opposite bank, its skull was split and it was dead. Then Fara Maka, who had seen the mighty throw, exclaimed, "What a daughter I have!"

Very soon, the whole tribe heard what had happened, and the Dialli, the minstrel folk, sang the song of Nana Miriam's adventure with the hippopotamus, which used to devastate the rice fields. And in the years that followed, no one in the Land of the Songai starved any more.

South Africa

MBEGA THE KIGEGO

The first king of the Shambala built his house on the mountain of Kilindi in the Land of Usambara, which is rich in fertile valleys, forests, and meadows. His son moved to Rabai and there his grandson lived too. The latter, like all the Shambala kings, had several wives and many children. His youngest wife was the mother of two sons, the younger of whom was called Mbega.

When Mbega reached the age at which a child cuts its teeth, the upper ones came through all together and before the lower ones. This is so unusual that such children are called *kigego* among the Shambala, and are believed to bring bad luck. No kigego might remain alive. They were all thrown into a deep ravine.

Mbega's mother did not dare to tell the king that his youngest son was a kigego. But the king noticed that she was concealing something and asked her, "What is worrying you?"

So she said, "I have given birth to a kigego. Mbega's upper teeth have come through first. What will you do?"

"I shall wait for the lower teeth, the lazy ones."

And so Mbega's life was spared. He grew into a strong handsome boy who was loved by everyone. Only his stepbrothers bore him a grudge and reproached him with being a kigego. And when the king and Mbega's brother both died, the stepbrothers often mentioned that a person who had been born under such an unlucky omen had no right to live. They did not invite him to their feasts and they cheated him out of his inheritance. When his mother died, they did not allow him to play his part at her funeral.

After this, Mbega crept away into the bush like an animal. Then he went to the elders of the tribe and besought them to go to his stepbrothers and to put three questions to them, "Why do you not give Mbega his share of the inheritance? Why do you never invite him to a feast? What has Mbega done to you?"

The stepbrothers winked at each other as the elders put these questions to them, and when they had finished, one of them said, "We are not surprised that you, and not Mbega himself, have come to us. Mbega does not exist. He is dead, since he is a kigego, which means bad luck for the whole tribe. There is no room in Rabai for such a one. We hope that you elders understand this, and that you do not come back to us a second time."

At this, the elders grew afraid and said, "We shall not come back a second time."

Mbega feasted the elders when they returned and waited for them to speak. But when he heard what his stepbrothers had decided, he said, "I shall have nothing more to do with them. I shall go away."

Now it happened that Mbega was well respected among the Shambala tribe. The young men especially, the ones who went hunting with him, were utterly devoted to him. Mbega had taught them how to hunt with dogs, which had not hitherto been the custom among the Shambala. The hunting dogs were a great help, for they feared neither lion nor leopard. Above all, they attacked the wild boar which used to descend upon Usambara in great herds and lay waste to the crops. No one knew better how to drive them from the fields than Mbega with his pack of dogs. Besides, he provided many families with meat.

Mbega had other qualities for which he was admired. He could read the future from the signs that appeared when he sprinkled a board with sand and moved it to and fro. He knew how to make magic with mists and with clouds. So he could have punished his stepbrothers as they deserved. But he did not even consider it, because they also were the sons of his father. "I will not shed their blood," he said, as his hunting companions urged him to do something about his stepbrothers.

He gave all his friends good hunting dogs and he went away from Rabai, the place where the ravine lay into which his stepbrothers would gladly have pushed him. He took with him nothing but his spear, bells for the dogs, the board on which he sprinkled sand, and the odds and ends he needed to make mist and cloud magic. And fourteen dogs as well. The finest of these was Chamsumu. Mbega called it "My Heart," because he could always rely on it.

On the evening of the second day, he came to the gate of the city of Kilindi, which was already locked for the night. He beat on the doors and cried, "I am Mbega!"

At first, the people refused to believe him, but presently they came to the gates and when they saw him and his fourteen dogs, they said, "It is he. It is Mbega, the mighty hunter who killed the wild boars."

They led him to their chief and the latter received him as a king's son and did everything to honor him. A house was prepared for his use, equipped with everything that he needed and laid with matting.

Mbega remained in Kilindi for several months. He rid the land of the wild beasts that were doing widespread damage. Then no one had reason to fear that a leopard would attack him by the roadside. Mbega also knew of many healing herbs and he cared for the sick. Everything he did increased the respect that the whole tribe felt for him. The chieftain's only son called him his brother.

One day it was reported to the chief that a large herd of wild boar had appeared only a few days' march from Kilindi. At once Mbega prepared to rid the neighborhood of them. The chief's son begged him, "Do take me with you!" But Mbega refused, for he knew that it was dangerous. The hunters too had their misgivings. But the chief's son turned to his father and he pestered him so long that at last he yielded and allowed the young man to take part in the hunt.

After three days, they came upon the wild boars. They were exceptionally big and powerful, and more dangerous than leopards. With their tusks they ripped deep furrows in the fields. Their grunting was louder than the roaring of lions when they are provoked.

With Mbega at their head, the hunters closed in and hurled their spears. Mbega's dogs attacked, digging their teeth into the boars' flesh. It was such a fierce battle, that some of the hunters lost their nerve and scrambled up trees. Five of them were wounded, but before long, almost all the wild boars were slain.

But when the men reassembled, the chief's son was missing. They called his name everywhere, but there was no answer. When at last they found him, they saw to their horror that he was dead. The others dared not return to Kilindi. They were sure that the chief would blame them and kill them all. After lengthy consultation, they decided to leave for Zirai. On the way they killed many wild beasts and were well received everywhere.

After some time, the Bumburi chief died and the elders of the tribe approached Mbega and offered him the chieftaincy. So Mbega joined them and he also took with him his hunters and his eleven surviving dogs. He married a girl of the Bumburi tribe and he became a chief who was respected for his kindness and his courage. His reputation rested most of all on his magic powers, although he seldom used them. He had no ambition to be mightier than others, nor to enlarge his dominion, the dream of almost all the other chiefs and kings.

Then the Vuga people, the biggest tribe in Usambara, were attacked by the warlike Para tribe, who wrought more destruction than even the most savage of wild boars. The Vuga people turned to Mbega, and they offered him the chieftaincy, if only he would put the Para tribe to flight. Mbega consulted his own men, and they agreed to make an alliance with the Vuga.

Mbega received the Vuga ambassadors outdoors. He wore a tanned oxhide and he was armed with club, sword and spear. The sky was cloudless, for the monsoon was blowing from the northeast, a scorching wind which makes it difficult to breathe. The Vuga ambassadors were amazed to see that Mbega was lighting a fire. Then he held a gourd over it and poured water on the embers, at the same time murmuring the magic for clouds. Steam arose which thickened into clouds, until at last they all sat in the shade of dense clouds, that protected them from the pitiless glare of the sun.

The story of the magic clouds spread quickly in all directions, and soon the Para heard of it too. They quickly withdrew into their own land, for they no longer dared to invade Vuga country, now that the latter had such a mighty chief.

When Mbega moved to the Vuga country, he took with him his Bumburi wife. Her brothers and four elders of the tribe were to be Mbega's advisers. On the way to the new palace, they rested several times and at one halt, a lion broke into their camp at night. The men were paralyzed with fear at the sight of the lion. But Mbega attacked it with his spear and killed it with a single stab through the heart.

It was only when the other men saw that the lion was dead that they ventured near it. Mbega did not reproach them. He merely told two of the men to remove the lion's skin. "I shall need it soon," said Mbega.

The next morning they traveled on and they reached the palace at midday. Drums were beaten and other drums answered from all the surrounding villages. The whole tribe assembled to greet their new chief who had routed the enemy without resort to arms. Mbega had many oxen slaughtered and he gave a great feast.

Then he had a new house built for himself. After six weeks, he sent for the lionskin. It was needed now because Mbega's wife was about to have a child, and Mbega wanted it to be born on the lionskin. Many Vuga women attended the chieftain's wife, and when the baby was born, cries of joy echoed through the land. People came from all parts, bringing gifts for it.

Runners came to Mbega to bring him the news and he asked them, "Is it a son or a daughter?"

"A son," said his wife's messengers.

"Are the boy and his mother well?"

"They are both very well."

"Has his mother picked a name for him yet?"

"She would like him to be called Buge, if you have no objection."

"I don't mind," said Mbega, "but I would like to give him another name as well if his mother does not mind."

"What name?" asked the messengers.

"He should be called Simba, the Lion, for he was born on a lionskin," said Mbega. "That is the name by which people shall greet him."

The baby's mother liked the name and Simba grew up to resemble it. He became a mighty hunter like his father. One day, ambassadors from the Bumburi tribe came to ask if Simba the Lion might become their chief. Mbega consented. Laughing, he said to the Bumburi ambassadors, "Your tribe gave me a girl. I send you a man in return!"

"A fair exchange," said the ambassadors, and they returned home with their young chieftain.

Central Africa

THE LEOPARD

Ki, the Pygmy, had married a Pygmy girl from another village. The girl was called Luetsi and she now became Ki's wife. With them lived Ntio, a brother of Ki's. After a year, Luetsi wished to visit her mother, as was the custom. Ki agreed and gave Luetsi a big piece of meat to take to her mother. As a big hunt was imminent, Ki could not go with his wife, but he promised to fetch her from her mother's in four weeks' time.

Now it happened that Ki was bitten in the foot by a snake and he could not walk. So he asked his brother to fetch his wife. Ntio did not want to go and said, "In a few days' time you will be able to walk again. It is better for you to fetch your wife yourself."

"No," said Ki. "It is better not to leave Luetsi in uncertainty. She would not wait for me but would start the journey home alone. Fetch her home for me, and I'll give you my best bow."

So Ntio went and fetched Luetsi. They took the path through the jungle, the woman ahead, the man, armed, close behind her, as was proper.

Suddenly, a leopard appeared among the trees, and it crouched ready to spring. The woman was paralyzed with fear. Ntio, however, threw himself on the leopard and thrust his knife into its heart. As it fell, the claws tore open Ntio's shoulder. Then the beast fell dead. Luetsi cleansed Ntio's wound, dressed it with healing herbs and put a bandage around it. Then she said, "You are brave, Ntio. You saved my life. I wonder if Ki would have done as much for me."

"You ought not to say such things," said Ntio.

But Luetsi continued, "One has heard of men who allowed their wives to be eaten by the leopard, while they themselves disappeared faster than a snake."

"Not my brother Ki," protested Ntio.

Then Luetsi said, "I have no child of his. It is because he does not love me enough."

"You shouldn't talk such nonsense," said Ntio. "He loves you. And he does not lack courage either. Perhaps he is the bravest of us three."

"Let's put it to the test!" said Luetsi suddenly.

"What do you mean?" inquired Ntio.

Eagerly Luetsi told him. "I shall lie down as if the leopard had jumped on me and pinned me to the ground. You roll the leopard over on top of me, so that it looks as if it is just going to eat me up. Then you run to Ki as fast as you can, tell him that the leopard has attacked me, and bring him here."

"Very well," said Ntio. He rolled the leopard over on top of the obstinate woman and then ran home to fetch his brother. However, as soon as Luetsi could no longer see him, he decided to take his time.

And so Luetsi had to lie there for hours, beneath the dead leopard. In the distance she could hear the roaring of the leopardess, looking for its dead mate. The jungle was full of threatening voices. At last she began to imagine that the leopard lying on top of her was moving, as if it had come to life again. But still she did not budge from the spot, so keen was she to find out how her husband would behave.

Meanwhile, Ntio had arrived at the village. He burst into the hut where his brother lay and repeated the words that Luetsi had told him. Ki sprang to his feet without delay, and in spite of his bad foot, he ran after his brother. Soon, indeed, he overtook him, and although he was unarmed, he threw himself on the leopard.

The woman rolled the dead beast over and stood up, laughing.

"What does this mean?" asked Ki.

"I wanted to see which of us was the greatest hero," said Luetsi.

And that is my question too, as we come to the end of the story: which of the three showed the greatest courage?

Was it Ntio, who stabbed the leopard in the heart with

his knife, although he could have run away? Or Luetsi, who lay there beneath the leopard? Or was it Ki, who ran up, unarmed, in order to snatch his wife from the leopard's claws?

ASIA AND AUSTRALIA

Polynesia

THE STOLEN FIRE

Maui lived at the time when mankind did not know about fire. So he, like everyone else, lived on raw meat and uncooked plants. One day, however, he had a visit from his mother Harva, who had lived among the gods for a long time. She brought with her a basket of cooked food. Maui ate some of it and he thought that it tasted much better than the food he was used to.

"You have brought good food with you," said Maui appreciatively.

"I am glad you enjoyed it," said Harva.

"But how is it that this meat and these vegetables taste so much better than those I usually eat?" inquired Maui.

"It is because they are cooked," said Harva.

"How are they cooked?"

"On a fire."

"Why didn't you bring any fire with you?" asked Maui.

"Because Mahuika guards it jealously," said Harva. "He

is the guardian of the fire, and he will never give a human being a burning spill of wood or a bowl of glowing embers."

"Is he powerful?" asked Maui.

"He is an invincible giant," said Harva. "No one has ever dared to seek him out. He would crush them to pieces."

Harva hoped that these words would frighten her son. But when she returned to the Land of the Gods, Maui followed her in secret. He saw that his mother stopped in front of a wall of rock and he heard her utter a magic spell. At once a gateway appeared in the rock, and Harva passed through it. Then the rock closed again behind her.

But Maui had remembered the magic words. He repeated them, and the wall of rock opened for him as it had done for Harva. Then he passed through the gateway and he came to a house where lived a kinsman of his mother's, a man named Tane.

Tane was friendly and offered Maui hospitality. Then Maui told him his plan.

"What you propose is dangerous," said Tane. "What drives you to such madness?"

"Why shouldn't men have fire? Why is it reserved for the gods?" asked Maui.

"You are courageous," said Tane. "I like that."

He gave Maui the red dove, Fearless, and he confided to him an incantation, which would turn Maui into a dragonfly.

"The dove Fearless will lead you through the Demon Gorge, and beyond it stands a house of banyan logs. There lives Mahuika, the guardian of the fire. But this I tell you—as you fly through the gorge, both you and the dove will be in great danger."

"I must have fire," said Maui.

Then Tane allowed him to go on.

Maui changed himself into a dragonfly, perched on the dove's back, and together they flew through the Demon Gorge. This gorge was as deep as a well, a dark, narrow alleyway cut through the rock. As soon as the dove flew inside, demon arms darted from the rocks and tried to grasp her with their red fingers. Zig-zagging wildly from side to side, she managed to evade the hands. The demons could not do more than pluck a few feathers from her tail.

As soon as the gorge was safely behind them, Maui turned himself into a man again. The dove returned to Tane. But Maui went on to the house of banyan logs, before which sat Mahuika, guardian of the fire. The giant looked up from the fire in amazement.

"Who are you?" he asked.

Maui told him his name.

"Where do you come from?"

"From the world of men."

"How did you pass through the Demon Gorge?"

"That is my secret," answered Maui. "But if you reveal to me your secret of making fire, I shall tell you mine in exchange."

Mahuika thought he could outwit Maui. He took a burning spill of wood from the fire and gave it to Maui, saying,

"Here you have all you need." For Mahuika thought, "This spill will have burned to nothing by the time Maui has passed through the gorge again."

But Maui saw through the trick and waited until the spill had burned itself out. Then Mahuika gave him a bowl of glowing embers. Maui took them into a pool of water, so that they went out with a hiss. This made Mahuika furious. He gave Maui hot ashes and shouted, "Be off with you now, or I'll trample you to dust!"

Maui tossed the hot ashes in the giant's face, so that he could not see. In vain he tried to grab hold of Maui.

"Now I could easily kill you with burning sticks of wood," said Maui, "but I want the secret from you. Wash the ash from your eyes. Let us fight fairly, man to man."

The giant agreed. He washed his face in the pool of water and got ready to fight. "You're very plucky for your size," he mocked, gazing scornfully at Maui.

"The biggest thing about you is your mouth," retorted Maui. "Come on, let's begin."

"All right, you dwarf!" roared Mahuika. He picked up Maui with one hand and, roaring with laughter, he tucked him into his broad belt.

The laughter, however, did not last long. Maui was in such an aggressive mood that he swelled out his chest, and the giant's belt snapped in two.

"First round to me," said Maui, as the giant picked up his belt in embarrassment. "But since you are so strong, you can easily uproot all the bushes that grow here."

"Why should I uproot them?"

"To give us more room for the second round."

So the giant cleared the ground and stamped it flat. Then he asked Maui, "How shall we amuse ourselves now?"

"With throwing," said Maui. "One will throw the other high into the air."

"I'll begin," said Mahuika.

"Come on then," cried Maui.

The giant seized him and threw him into the air. Maui came down into Mahuika's hands. The giant threw him a second time, shouting, "Ho ho ho, up you go, ever so high!" The third time, Maui remained in the air so long that the giant had time to sing a whole song. This is what he sang—

Up you go to the first level
Up you go to the second level
Up you go to the third level
Up you go to the fourth level
Up you go to the fifth level
Up you go to the sixth level
Up you go to the seventh level
Up you go to the eighth level
Up you go to the ninth level
Up you go to the tenth level!

Then the giant stopped and stared at Maui, who was still in the air. "Come on, it's time you dropped!" he shouted. But still Maui did not fall. He paddled with his hands through the air, and then landed on his feet, beside Mahuika, saying, "That was great fun. Now it's your turn."

"What!" exclaimed the giant. "Do you think you can throw a whale like me into the air?"

"I can try," said Maui. And he seized the giant and tossed him into the air. The first time Mahuika flew as high as the coconut tree. The second, he flew as high as the date palm. At the third throw, Maui sang the same song that Mahuika had sung, the song of the ten levels.

Up you go to the first level
Up you go to the second level
Up you go to the third level
Up you go to the fourth level
Up you go to the fifth level
Up you go to the sixth level
Up you go to the seventh level
Up you go to the eighth level
Up you go to the ninth level
Up you go to the tenth level!

And then Maui sang the magic Song of Remaining in the Air. And as long as Maui went on singing it, Mahuika could not return to earth.

"Let me come down!" howled the giant.

"If I let you fall, you'll be smashed to pulp," Maui warned him.

"No, no!" cried the giant, terrified. "Leave me up here!"

"Then you'll starve to death," laughed Maui. "Is that what you want?"

"Then catch me," begged the giant. "And in return, I'll show you how to make fire."

"That's all I want," said Maui. He caught Mahuika in his arms and not a hair of the giant's head was injured.

Mahuika went into the house of banyan logs. He came out again with two fire sticks, one round and the other flat, with a small hollow in it. The giant placed the round stick in the little hole and twirled it between the palms of his hands. After a short time, to Maui's astonishment, a tongue of flame shot out.

"That is good," said Maui.

So Mahuika gave him the two pieces of wood for making fire, and a blazing torch as well. "Since you have defeated me, the Demon Gorge cannot hurt you any longer," he told Maui.

So Maui returned happily to the world of men. He taught them the art of making fire and henceforth they could eat cooked food like the gods and warm themselves by the fireside. They observed too that the fire kept wild animals at a safe distance, and so it guarded them from danger as well. Maui discovered that metals were easier to work with the help of fire, and that it hardened mud into brick. And so fire became the assistant of mankind and its servant.

But whenever a man made a fire, he used to sing a song as he did so, the magic Song of Remaining in the Air that Maui had composed about Mahuika. The fire-giant was punished by the gods, who said he had betrayed them, but Maui praised him as someone who had fought a clean fight.

ETANA'S FLIGHT TO HEAVEN

Of the many kings of Sumer, none cared so well for his people as Etana, who was known as "The Good Shepherd." He killed the lions that broke into farmsteads to steal the livestock and threaten the children. Whoever was in trouble could turn to the king for help.

Once the Eagle of Heaven sought him out and asked him for help. Whenever the bird left its nest in order to find food, it had reason to fear that a snake would devour its young.

So Etana climbed the mountain and pursued the snake until he found it. He fought with it for a long time, but at last he strangled it and stamped on its head.

The only person Etana could not help was his wife, who risked her life every time she gave birth to a child.

One day, when the queen was expecting another baby, Etana went to the temple to consult the god Enlil. Enlil told the king that the herb of easy childbirth was only for the gods. But at the same time, he revealed to Etana the exact spot where it grew in Heaven.

Etana left the temple downcast. How could he mount to Heaven without wings? Then he remembered the eagle, whose enemy he had destroyed. He sought the eagle in its aerie and said to it, "My queen will soon give birth to another child. I do not want her to suffer, nor do I want her life to be endangered. Enlil has told me where the herb of easy childbirth grows in Heaven. I want to fetch it, if you will carry me there."

The eagle agreed, because Etana had saved its young. It grasped the king and lifted him into the air. Etana looked down, and he saw the rivers dwindling to threads, the Land of Sumer became a tiny patch of ground. Then Etana felt afraid and his heart grew empty. The king clutched the eagle's neck and cried, "Go back!" The eagle did as Etana bid and carried the king down to earth.

Etana did not dare enter his palace. Instead, he went to the temple to confess to the god Enlil that he had failed in his attempt. The king was full of grief, for he knew the ordeal his wife had to face.

Enlil comforted him, saying, "It is true that men are born in pain, but that is how they conquer death. And even if you did not succeed in your aim, at least you dared to try."

Then Etana returned to his palace. On the way, he was greeted with the news that the queen had given birth to a son.

India

MUCHUKUNDA AND KRISHNA

In ancient times, a mighty king named Muchukunda reigned in the Land of the Hindus. He was so victorious in battle, so strong in armed conflict, that even the gods asked him for his assistance when they were hard pressed. And he helped the gods to win a glorious victory. In return, they offered to grant him any wish he cared to make.

Muchukunda asked for time to think. What could such a great monarch wish for? He had land enough and wealth enough. He was fortunate in everything he undertook. He had a wife and sons who loved him, and he towered above all other mortal men.

When the time had elapsed, the gods asked him for the second time to make a wish. By now, Muchukunda was weary of battle. After his last victory he was so exhausted that he desired nothing but to rest for as long as he wished. So he retreated like a bear into a cave and he said to the gods, "My wish is to sleep away the rest of my time, for I am tired out. I don't want anyone to wake me, and should someone do so, let him burst into flames at my first glance, and turn to ashes before my eyes."

The gods granted him his wish, and the old king Muchukunda fell into a deep sleep.

Muchukunda slept in the heart of the mountains, concealed in the cave. Time went by. Many kings succeeded each other and many wars were waged. Songs were sung of Muchukunda, for no king was considered his equal. He was said to have made his home among the gods. No one knew that he was still lying in a cave, fast asleep.

So things remained until Krishna, the son of the gods, became king in the Land of the Hindus. He knew the cave where King Muchukunda slept. He also knew that whoever woke the king from his slumber would burst into flames at the first glance and be turned to ashes.

Krishna fought and defeated the demons who threatened his country, and then a time of peace for India set in which lasted for many years. Then a barbarian king invaded the land. His armies laid waste to the crops. Krishna advanced to meet the enemy with only a small army. When his soldiers saw the great might of the barbarians, they were afraid and wanted to run away. But Krishna said, "Stay here and have no fear. You will not need to fight. Not a man shall lose his life, nor even receive a wound. I shall decide the battle single-handed and this is the right place for it."

Krishna went forth alone towards the invading army and he challenged the king to come and fight with him. The barbarian king stepped forward fully armed and his shield-bearer followed.

"Where are your weapons?" he asked Krishna.

"I need none," was the answer.

"How can you defeat me then?" asked the barbarian.

"By running away," replied Krishna.

And he started running towards the nearby mountain where Muchukunda slept.

The king of the barbarians pursued him, with the shield-bearer following behind. They raced across the plain and Krishna darted into the cave. And because he had a big lead, he had time to hide himself close to the sleeping Muchukunda.

When the barbarian king entered the cave, he was out of breath. He ordered his shield-bearer to light a torch and they saw a man asleep. The king kicked the sleeper and Muchukunda awoke. His eyes opened and he stared at the intruder. Aghast, the shield-bearer saw his master burst into flames and turn to ashes before his eyes. He ran for his life, and as soon as he reached his fellow countrymen and reported the death of the king, the barbarian hordes turned and fled. They left India and never dared to attack it again.

Krishna stepped up to Muchukunda and bowed low. "Thank you for saving my country," he said. "My army was not strong enough to come to grips with the enemy. Forgive me for intruding."

"Now I am awake again, I feel myself dragged into the whirlpool where all living things swirl round and round," said Muchukunda. "But my only wish is to have done with it all."

He and Krishna left the cave, and when they came to the Hindu army, Muchukunda was amazed to see how small the men were. He walked like a giant in their midst.

"What am I doing here?" asked Muchukunda. He turned and made for the high mountains, remote from all mankind, there to live until his time came.

Sakhalin

KUTUNE SHIRKA AND THE GOLDEN OTTER

Kutune Shirka and his brother Otopush lived with their stepbrother and stepsister, who had brought up the two brothers. Otopush and the stepbrother were armorers. The stepsister was skilled in magic.

Kutune Shirka used to sit in the corner by the stove. He liked looking at the precious swords, the armor, and the equipment used for making magic. He himself took a delight in carving animals to decorate sheaths and shields, above all bears and lions, which he succeeded in making most lifelike. When he was not carving, he would sit there doing nothing. Yet he had the stature of a hero.

Now at that time, the Golden Otter reappeared at the mouth of the Ishkar River. It had not shown itself there for many a long year. The Man of Ishkar, the prince whose castle stood at the mouth of the river, sent messages to the bravest Ainu heroes, telling them to come and capture the

Golden Otter for him. The man who did so should marry the prince's daughter.

The stepsister heard about this summons, and she urged Kutune Shirka, "Go and catch the Golden Otter!"

"Why me?" he asked, going on with his carving.

"Because it is your destiny," the stepsister insisted. "I saw in a dream that you caught the Golden Otter."

Kutune Shirka did not believe her. He carved away at the figure of a lion for the sheath of a sword that he had already decorated with five lions. The stepsister ran up and down in excitement, and tried to prod him into action. But he had eyes only for his lions and as he finished the last one, he said, "Now I have six lions! Are they not alive?"

The lions were crouching for the spring, but the stepsister ignored them. "I saw in a dream how you caught the otter," she repeated.

That night, Kutune Shirka woke up suddenly. He felt that someone had been shaking him, but when he looked around, he could see no one, although it was light indoors and the weapons gleamed. His brothers and sister lay fast asleep. Kutune Shirka stretched his arms and with one bound, he jumped out of bed. He went to a chest, took out an embroidered coat and a belt with golden clasps. Then he put on a golden helmet, slipped a sword into the sheath with the six lions and fastened it securely to his belt. He squared his shoulders and felt so pleased with life that he began dancing like a bear. Suddenly he felt a great desire to go forth and do great deeds. He determined to catch the

Golden Otter, but for himself, and not for the Man of Ishkar.

Without hesitation, he set out. His brothers and sister noticed nothing of his leaving. He stepped outside the door and for the first time in his life, he saw the house from the outside. "So this is the castle where I grew up," he thought, full of joy. "And all this time I had no idea how splendid it is. The fence is not broken, but high and straight, a white and not a black cloud, the posts are firmly rammed into the ground. Below there is room for the mice to nest, and above there is space for the birds. The wind can blow between the rails and make music as it whistles through. And the door is a mouth that bids one welcome, the roof is a hat to keep out the snow and the rain. What a fine house it is!"

The paths that led to the house sparkled in the starlight. Kutune Shirka picked the one that led to the Ishkar River, to the castle by the sea. The god who was his guardian thundered over his head and gave him the stride of a giant, so that he reached the shore as day was breaking. A sea breeze blew in his face, and wrinkled the surface of the water like a reed mat. The waterfowl tucked their heads under their tails, then bobbed them out again, chattering to each other.

The other heroes who wanted to catch the Golden Otter had already assembled at the castle. From the window of the tower, the Woman of Ishkar looked out. Strands of hair hung from her chin, which was as sharp as a crust of bread.

The look in her eyes betrayed her greed for the Golden Otter, which kept rising from the water, glistening like a sword. The Woman of Ishkar did not take her eyes off the heroes.

The first to try was the Man from the East. He saluted the Woman of Ishkar, who gave him a sneer and waggled her chin. Then he dived into the water, down to the depths. Twice, thrice, he made to grasp the otter, chasing it with outstretched arms. But soon he grew short of breath and he had to turn back. The waves cast him up on the shore, where he lay gasping.

Next the Man from the Far Island tried, and after him the Man from the Little Island. Both were men who had performed many deeds, but both had to give up because the otter dived too deep.

The Woman of Ishkar poured scorn on these failures.

Then it was Kutune Shirka's turn. He did not glance at the Woman of Ishkar, but leaped into the surf. At first the Golden Otter seemed not to know who was in pursuit. Twice it eluded Kutune Shirka's grasp. But when Kutune Shirka followed it down to the bottom of the sea and placed his foot on it, the Golden Otter recognized him. At once it swam into his arms and drew him to the surface.

Kutune Shirka still had breath enough to scramble up onto the shore: The Golden Otter remained in his arms, and gave him strength to leap forward in great bounds. Before the Woman of Ishkar could leave her tower, Kutune Shirka had already reached home.

He placed the Golden Otter on the chest beside the articles used for sacrificing to the gods. The otter gleamed more brightly than all the vessels and weapons. But when the stepbrother saw what Kutune Shirka had brought home, he said angrily, "Now the peace that has reigned for so long in this house will come to an end. Many men have already lost their lives for the sake of this otter. It had disappeared. Why did it come to light again? And why were you the one who had to catch it? The Man of Ishkar will take his revenge."

And so it happened. There began a long quarrel which grew to a clash of arms. Many men took sides. Many lost their lives in the fighting.

The survivors agreed on a truce, and the brothers invited all the combatants to come to a banquet. Apart from the brothers, there were four more heroes left alive. The Man from Iyochi, the Man from Rupetom, the Man from Shamput and the Man from Ruvesami. All were praised for their great deeds.

The brothers and their guests dined merrily when suddenly they heard the ring of approaching footsteps. Two giants had descended from the mountains and were heading towards the house. This sobered everyone immediately. The men seized their weapons and stepped out to do battle. The two giants came nearer. With every step their feet sank into the earth as if they were tramping through deep snow. The Men of Iyochi, Rupetom, Shamput and Ruvesami were all terrified and ran away.

The brothers went out to meet the giants. The stepbrother and Otopush took on one of them, and Kutune Shirka the other. The fight was a hard one. When sword met sword, lightning flashed. The two giants stood their ground like rocks, their arms did not grow tired.

Otopush was the first to fall. Then the stepbrother was felled as a tree is uprooted by a hurricane. Now the two giants circled around Kutune Shirka and he was hard pressed. In despair, he grasped the sheath on which he had carved six lions. They all came to life and three tackled each of the giants. It was not difficult then for Kutune Shirka to lay low his adversaries.

The stepsister hurried to the scene and attended to her brother and Otopush, who were both still alive. Slowly they regained their senses and, after three days, they had recovered.

After his victory over the giants, no one ever again dared to challenge Kutune Shirka's possession of the Golden Otter.

Japan

ISANAGI AND ISANAMI

When the gods were still busy with the creation of the earth, they gave Isanagi and Isanami the task of setting a chain of islands in the sea. The gods gave them precious spears to take with them. Isanagi and Isanami stood on the bridge between Heaven and earth and they stirred the sea so hard that it made a noise like this: *kovorro-kovorro-kovorro*. Gradually the water turned into a thick broth, and the broth hardened into solid ground which bonded with the sea-bed. That was how the island of Onogoro came into being. Isanagi and Isanami made Onogoro into the main pillar for all the other lands, they built a palace there and lived on Onogoro as man and wife.

For their sons and daughters they created smaller islands, to which they sent their children in reed boats. The islands were called after the children: Sweet Prince, Prince Well-Cooked Rice, Princess Dainty Dishes, Prince Brave

Boy and there were seven other equally delightful names.

The youngest prince was called Prince Firelight and Isanami died at his birth. Isanagi was beside himself with grief. He would not reconcile himself to the fact of Isanami's death and defying all the warnings, he set out for the Land of the Dead to fetch her back. He descended to the underworld and he beat on its gates. "Isanami! Isanami! Isanami!" he called so loudly that the underworld trembled. Then he heard Isanami's voice.

"What do you want?" she asked. "Why do you wake me?"

"Because the lands that you and I were to make are not yet finished," said Isanagi. "You must come back."

"You have come too late," said Isanami. "I have eaten too much of the food that is served in the Land of the Dead. But I am so overwhelmed by your coming that I shall speak to those who rule this realm and ask them to release me."

She turned to the rulers and said, "Give me a sign that you are listening."

Then the gate of the underworld flew open.

Isanami said quickly, "Do not look at me, Isanagi. Otherwise all will be lost."

Isanagi turned away and waited while Isanami went to the rulers of the Land of the Dead. A long time passed and she did not return. Isanagi was distraught with grief. He took a comb from his knot of hair, broke off a tooth and set it alight. With this as a torch he entered the Land of the Dead and looked everywhere. Suddenly he saw Isanami coming towards him, but her body had already started to decay. Horrified at her appearance, he recoiled and clapped his hands to his face.

"Why could you not wait for me?" said Isanami. "At the gate, I would have been restored to life. But now that you have seen me in a state of decay, we must part for ever, and my love for you is changed to hatred."

Then Isanagi turned and fled. But Isanami summoned the Ugly One to pursue him. Isanagi saw her coming and tore off his headcloth and threw it behind him. It changed into a vine, and the Ugly One sat down until she had eaten all the grapes. Then she took up the chase once more.

Next Isanagi broke off all the teeth of his comb and threw them behind him. Hundreds of bamboo shoots sprang up and the Ugly One stopped to pick and eat them. So she lost sight of Isanagi.

Then Isanami took up the pursuit of Isanagi herself. She caught up with him at the pass that marks the frontier. Beside it stood a peach tree laden with ripe fruit. Isanagi threw the peaches at his sister-wife. She stopped and picking up a rock, she hurled it. The rock lay between them, parting them for ever.

"Now we are enemies, you alive and I dead," cried Isanami.

"Why must it be so?" asked Isanagi in despair.

"Because you were too bold and would not wait," said Isanami. "As your punishment, I shall make a thousand of your people die every day."

"That is not a mortal blow," answered Isanagi. "Every day two thousand children will be born."

Then Isanami realized that no matter how powerful were the Lords of the Underworld, the living would always prevail.

Tibet

KESAR OF LING AND THE GIANT OF THE NORTH

Kesar, the son of the ruler of Ling, was so ugly at his birth that all who saw him recoiled in horror. His mouth was as big as the opening of a well, and his eyes were grim. The child could stand as soon as he was born, and when he found nothing to eat but moldy grain, he ate it, moldy as it was. His mother, Queen Gongza, said, "He hasn't begun to grow, and yet here he is, stuffing himself with moldy grain."

The queen was so ashamed of her child that she did not want to rear him. She wrapped him in an ass's skin, tied a rope of goat's hair around it and weighed it down with a stone. But Karthigmo, her mother, came to her and said, "You have given birth to a baby. What kind of child is it?"

"I have given birth to a monster," said the queen. "He is so greedy that he stuffed his mouth with grain the moment he was born. So I have wrapped him in an ass's skin, tied it with a goat's hair rope and placed a heavy stone upon it."

"How could you do such a thing!" exclaimed the queen's mother. "If your husband the king were still alive, he would surely punish you."

She took the bundle from under the stone, untied the goat's hair rope, unwrapped the child from the ass's skin and gave him the name of Kesar.

The child looked bright-eyed at Karthigmo, and with his mouth as big as a well, he said:

You are kinder than water, Mother Karthigmo;
now listen to me!
You are kinder than my own mother; now listen to me!
You have given me a name; now listen to me!
Does not a mother wrap her child in a sleeping-bag?
But mine wrapped me in an ass's skin.
She said she had born a greedy monster
A deformed monster with a mouth like a well.
A king's son has been born to her, say I.
White ribbons should flutter in the sky,
Red ribbons should flutter on the earth,
Blue ribbons should flutter over the sea.

The queen was alarmed when she heard this. But Karthigmo rejoiced.

Now a certain King Agu learned of the birth of the king's son and this king was eager to rule the Land of Ling. He said to the seven priests of the east, "If you can kill the child Kesar, I shall give you half my country."

So the priests disguised themselves as beggars and went to Queen Gongza, saying, "We do not come to beg, nor do we ask for a plate of gold or of silver. We are wise men. Let us have your child, so that we may educate him."

The queen gave them the child, and the beggar-priests took it with them.

When Karthigmo arrived, she asked where the child was.

"Seven wise men wished to educate Kesar, so I gave them the child. They took him away with them."

"How could you do such a thing!" said Karthigmo angrily.

So the queen ran after the beggar-priests and she found them in a hut. They had bound the child with chains, they had lit a fire beneath his heart, and they were pouring boiling water into his mouth.

When the mother saw this, she screamed, "Give me back my child!"

But Kesar, the king's son, said unconcerned:

Chains of iron I do not feel,
A bad sign for my enemies
The fire at my heart I do not feel
For the joy in my heart is too hot
The boiling water I do not feel
I shall live to drink milk
And tea in plenty.

Then Kesar said, "*Hoong* one! *Hoong* two!" And the chains fell in pieces, the fire turned to ash. The priests, however, were changed into beetles and made to eat the ash.

When Kesar was seven years old, King Agu himself went to Queen Gongza and said, "Where have you hidden your son?"

"Here I am!" cried Kesar, leaping out of bed. King Agu seized him with both hands and spun him round and round. Then he tried to lean out of the window and dash the child against a rock. But Kesar held on so tightly that Agu could not do as he wished. "Swing me, swing me, swing me hard!" shouted Kesar. "Dash me against the rock!"

And he would not let go.

Presently, when King Agu was exhausted, Kesar seized the man and whirled him round and round in the air. Then he threw him out of the window, so that he was dashed against the rocks.

King Agu tried to take Kesar's life many times after that, but he was always unsuccessful. There was only one creature who could be dangerous to Kesar, and that was the Giant of the North, whom everyone hated, and who ate human flesh. He had snatched the king's daughter Dzemo, and had forced her to be his wife. When Kesar heard this, he decided to free the king's daughter and kill the Giant of the North.

Kesar mounted his white horse. He rode through a black valley and across a black plain until he came to a black pass, where he found a black altar that the Giant of the North had erected. Kesar overturned the altar and demolished it. Then he came upon the flocks of sheep and goats that the Giant of the North had stolen. Kesar beckoned to the shepherds and he questioned them about the giant and the king's daughter Dzemo. At first the shepherds were too frightened to speak, but at last one of them said, "Since you are the King of Ling, I shall tell you what I know. The king's daughter Dzemo sits in an iron cage in the giant's castle. When you arrive there, you will find sentries at each gate, two giants who sit astride great elephants. But the giants and the elephants are dead. Therefore do not be afraid, but open the gates and enter."

Kesar arrived at the castle, and when he saw the dead giants, he showered them with arrows. They did not move and Kesar shuddered. He opened seven gates one after the other, until he came to the last gateway that was made of gold. Behind it was the room with the iron cage, where the king's daughter Dzemo sat.

"Who are you?" she asked him.

And when he told her his name, she said, "Misguided young man, this is the palace of the Giant of the North. How will you escape from his clutches?"

Kesar freed the king's daughter from the cage and asked, "When will the Giant of the North return?"

"We must wait until the wind rises," answered the king's daughter.

After two weeks, a gale arose and all the gates rattled on their hinges.

"What is this?" asked Kesar, alarmed.

"The Giant of the North is on his way home. The wind is the sign that he is halfway here."

"Where shall we hide, my horse and I?" asked Kesar.

Dzemo hastily took from her pocket seven small shells and seven small bones. *"Haha, huhu, hrumhrum!"* she said, and the bones and shells turned into moles. They began to dig a hole in the courtyard of the palace, as a hiding place for Kesar and his horse.

Hardly were they safely hidden and the king's daughter back in her cage, when the Giant of the North returned, carrying the horses and the men he had killed. "I'm hungry," he announced and promptly devoured five horses.

Then he turned to the king's daughter. "How shall I sleep?" he asked her. "Like a bird or like a stone?"

The king's daughter replied, "On the road, one should sleep like a bird. At home, like a stone."

"You are right," said the giant, who was very tired. He settled down and slept as soundly as if he intended to sleep for a whole year. Then Dzemo brought the bones and the shells and said, *"Haha, huhu, hrumhrum!"* And fourteen moles dug Kesar and his horse out of the ground.

The Giant of the North snored so loudly that the gates shook.

Kesar was trembling with fear. But the king's daughter said, "You need not be afraid. The giant will not awake. You can ride your horse up and down his body."

So Kesar rode his horse three times up and down the

huge body and the Giant of the North did not even move.

"Now you can kill him," said the king's daughter, "but remember that the monster has nine lives."

So Kesar set about depriving the giant of all his nine lives. There was a life in each of the big canine teeth that stuck out of his mouth and Kesar broke them off.

"What's happening?" mumbled the Giant of the North, and he turned over, but did not awaken.

Kesar cut off an arm and a foot, and they accounted for two more lives.

"Oh, do let me sleep," the giant growled and turned on his back.

Then it was the turn of both his ears, and two more lives were taken.

"Ouch!" shouted the Giant of the North, who had now lost six of his lives. But he still wanted to go on sleeping.

Kesar removed another arm and another foot, the seventh and the eighth of the giant's lives. And it was only then that the monster raised his head and shouted angrily, "Who is it who keeps disturbing my sleep?"

"King Kesar of Ling," said the king's daughter.

"Who released you from the iron cage?"

"King Kesar of Ling."

Then the giant saw that his arms and feet, his teeth and his ears had all been cut off. Fearfully he said, "Now I know that it is King Kesar of Ling who has taken eight of my lives."

"He will have your ninth life too," said Dzemo, handing

over the giant's sword. Then Kesar of Ling cut off the giant's head. He threw the iron cage into a ravine and overturned the dead elephants and the giants, so that anyone could enter the castle of the Giant of the North without being afraid.

But as for the king's daughter Dzemo, he took her back with him to Ling.

Australia

GIRROWIN

At the beginning of time, Bayami, the creator of the world, lived among men, and the earth was a garden. There were countless bushes and trees in blossom. For many months of the year, the ground was a carpet of flowers. Men lived happy and content. One day, however, a man began to criticize Bayami. "Bayami calls us his children," he said, "yet he allows us to die, while he remains immortal. Why may we not eat the fruit of the trees of life that grow in his garden?"

"Bayami has given us enough trees of other kinds," retorted an old man.

"You are right," answered the rebel. "He has indeed given us other trees, but whoever eats of them must die. Our Father feeds himself on fruits that give him alone eternal life. Is it not so?"

"Yes, you are right," others joined in.

"Then let us go and make Bayami explain," demanded the ringleader, and all the others followed him.

When they came into Bayami's presence, they asked him, "How can you call us your children, when you condemn us to die, while you live for ever?"

Bayami said nothing.

"Why are you allowed to do something that we are forbidden?" continued the ringleader. And going up to one of the three trees, he picked a fruit and ate it.

As if struck by lightning, he collapsed, dead.

Bayami, however, walked away in silence. He went to the Ubi Ubi Mountains, and climbing along a narrow path, he reached the Land of Peace and Quiet, which lay beyond the highest peak.

Then all the flowers died, the plains and the mountain-sides were bare, the trees and the bushes faded to the same drab hue. Since there were no blossoms left on earth, the bees died too, except for three hives, whose bees fed on the flowers of Bayami's trees. The people did not know what to do. They all blamed the man who had eaten the forbidden fruit.

"It is because of him that Bayami has abandoned us," they said angrily. "It is his fault that the earth has no flowers now. It all came about because he offended the creator."

"Didn't we all go to Bayami with him?" said the old man.

Then the others turned away from him and left him

alone. But like Bayami, the old man went into the Ubi Ubi Mountains, and he came to the foot of the highest peak that no one had ever climbed. The path was only a hand's breadth, and the mountainsides were white and steep. The old man shook off his fear and began the ascent. After five hours, he discovered a spring in a crack in the rock and when he had drunk this water, his weariness vanished.

From the mountain peak, he stepped through a gateway into the sky. There stood Bayami on an endless carpet of flowers. The old man was speechless with joy. But Bayami spoke, "You have done what no one before you dared to do. Take this handful of seeds and scatter them over the earth."

The old man took the seeds and carried them safely back to earth. He started sowing them, and his hand was never empty. Flowers bloomed everywhere. And the place where he had begun his sowing was covered with flowers as thick as the hairs in an opossum's fur. And even today, the place is known as Girrowin. That means the Place of Flowers.

China

THE PRINCE OF THE HOUSE OF LIU

One day, the sixth emperor of the House of Liu was suddenly taken very ill. So he called his twelve-year-old son to his bedside and said to him, "I shall not sit upon the Dragon Throne much longer. After my death, you will be in great danger. As you are so young, others will try to seize power and rule here. It is better, therefore, if you flee from Peking. In Nan Yang, there lives a man for whom I have done much. He will receive you well and hide you until your time comes. Go to old Chang. Everyone in Nan Yang knows him."

Soon afterwards, the sixth emperor of the House of Liu died. As he had foreseen, the prince was in great danger. Wang Mang, one of the emperor's kinsmen and also his prime minister, devised a plot to make himself emperor. And in order to dispel suspicion, he sent the street urchins of Peking singing through the city:

Sooner will copper horses grow from bamboo
Than Wang Mang seize the imperial throne.

And even as the boys outside were singing these words as loudly as they could, Wang Mang seized power in the Inner Palace and declared himself emperor.

By this time, the prince had already fled from Peking. For three days he wandered northwards. Then he grew uncertain and began wondering if he really had taken the right road to Nan Yang. When darkness fell, he sat down on a flat rock and he fell asleep, sitting upright.

That night, old Chang's son dreamed that he saw a youth sitting on a rock that he knew well, because it was not far from the city. He awoke and waited until his father rose next morning. Then he told him of his strange dream.

Old Chang spoke, "The youth whom you have seen in your dream is the Prince of the House of Liu. I knew that he had fled from the palace, but I did not know where he had gone. The Dragon Throne is his by right. Go to the flat rock and bring him here. Only do not say a word of this to anyone."

The son obeyed his father. He went to the flat rock and there sat the prince with great dignity. The son of old Chang bowed low and led him to his father's house. As soon as old Chang saw the prince, he performed the dance of homage before him. He kept the prince in his own house and no one knew the great secret.

But the usurper had proclaimed throughout the land that

the Prince of the House of Liu had fled in order to raise a rebellion against the new emperor. One hundred villages together with their inhabitants were offered in exchange for the prince's capture. And all who helped him were threatened with dire punishment.

The proclamation was also made in Nan Yang. At every sentry post a drum was hung, but one which was covered with soft cloth instead of skin. Only a real emperor or his heir could make such a drum sound. An ordinary man could never make it speak. A guard was set beside each of the cloth drums, and he had to stop all passers-by and make them beat the drum.

In this way, Wang Mang felt sure that he would find the prince. Many people beat the cloth drums, but never a sound was heard. One day, a youth walked past the drum in Nan Yang, and ignored the order to strike it. The guard seized the lad and shouted, "Why don't you stop and beat the drum, as the emperor has commanded?"

"If I did," the boy replied, "terrible things would happen."

"What kind of terrible things?" the guard asked.

"If I strike it once, all the other drums in the land will sound. If I strike it twice, all the rivers will rise. And if I strike it three times, heaven and earth will grow dark."

And as he spoke, the prince beat the drum three times, and darkness covered heaven and earth for several hours. Under its cover, it was easy for the prince to make his escape from the town.

The next day, the prince met a peasant plowing his field. Far and wide there was no one else to be seen. The prince walked boldly up to the peasant and said to him, "I am the Prince of the House of Liu, whom the usurper Wang Mang wants to capture. The proclamation hangs beside every sentry post. Soldiers in armor are pursuing me. Can you find me a safe hiding place?"

Without speaking, the peasant quickly dug a hole in the middle of the field. It was three feet deep and as long as a man. Even without words the prince understood him, and he lay down in the hole. The peasant placed seven grains of rice in the prince's mouth and put a long bamboo cane between his lips. Then he covered the prince with earth. But the prince could breathe through the hollow bamboo tube, and if he ate a grain of rice a day, he could survive for seven days.

When the soldiers who were after him failed to find him, they went to the Grand Astrologer and questioned him. The wise man gave them the following information, "The prince who fled lies three feet beneath the earth. Centipedes crawl from his mouth and a bamboo cane grows from his eye socket. That is what I have to tell you."

The soldiers said that they were satisfied and their captain gave Wang Mang the news. He was richly rewarded. The usurper gave orders for all the proclamation posters to be taken down, so that the people would forget all about the prince.

Then the peasant dug the prince out of his grave. The

prince asked the man for his advice. Then the peasant broke his silence and said, "Above the mountain Kun Lun stands the Great White Star. This is the star you must consult. It is not enough for you to trust the swiftness of your feet, the strength in your arms and the courage in your heart. Listen to the star!"

The prince scaled the mountain Kun Lun and consulted the Great White Star. Then he assembled a small army, as the star had advised him, and marched on the capital. The star had told him to take only a handful of warriors when he confronted Wang Mang.

As soon as the people recognized the Prince of the House of Liu, they flocked to join his army and so it grew. Even the palace guards hurried to join him. The usurper Wang Mang committed suicide. Thus it happened that the prince mounted the throne that his father had bequeathed to him. He appointed the peasant who knew how to hold his tongue and the old man Chang to be his advisers. And old Chang's son was also brought to the imperial court.

India

PRINCE FIVE-WEAPONS

The chief wife of the King of Benares bore her lord a son. The king rejoiced and on the day of the name-giving, he summoned the wisest men in the land to be present. They agreed to observe the child, until they could tell the nature of his being. At last one of the sages said, "Exalted king, your son has been given great gifts for his path upon this earth. He will succeed you as king. He will be first in Benares, in the Land of the Rose-Apple. He will be famous for the deeds he performs with five weapons."

And so the king named his son Prince Five-Weapons.

The prince grew up in his father's court. When he was sixteen years old, the king said to him, "It is time you were instructed in the art of using weapons. Go to the town of Takkasila. There anyone will tell you where you can find the finest teacher in the land."

Prince Five-Weapons went to Takkasila. And the famous Master instructed him and taught him everything he could. In the end, the prince knew as much as his teacher. As a parting gift, the latter gave him five weapons. The prince bowed deeply and departed from the town of Takkasila, to take the road back to Benares.

After a few days, he came to a forest where lived a great ogre, Sticky-Hair. The people who dwelled nearby warned the prince about the ogre, saying, "It is better to skirt the forest and go the long way around. The ogre Sticky-Hair devours everyone who enters the forest. No one has ever come out of it alive."

But Prince Five-Weapons was as fearless as the bearded lion. He had confidence in the five weapons that his teacher had given him. So he proceeded along the path that led through the forest.

When he reached the heart of the forest, the ogre Sticky-Hair came out and barred the prince's way. This ogre was as tall as a palm tree, his head was like a summerhouse with a bell-shaped pinnacle, his eyes were as big as wheels. The most terrifying thing about him were his two tusks, which were as thick as branches. He had a monstrous beak like a bird of prey. Lichens and mosses grew on his arms and legs and his belly was scarred with blotches. His body was covered with matted hair.

This repulsive creature shouted at the prince, "Where are you going?"

"To Benares."

"Never!" said the ogre. "I shall devour you, just as I have everyone else who has entered my forest."

"You had better step aside," said Prince Five-Weapons. "I come from the Master of Takkasila, and the weapons he has given me are more than a match for you."

"We'll soon see about that," shrieked the ogre, seizing the prince.

"I have fifty arrows, whose tips have been dipped in a poison that kills in an instant," the prince warned the ogre. "And I shall not miss when I shoot."

The prince drew his bow and hit the monster, but the arrow was caught in the thick hair and it did not pierce his hide. All his fifty arrows did the prince shoot at the ogre and fifty times they found their mark. But they all became entangled in the ogre's matted hair and they could not wound the monster.

Then the prince hurled his spear, which was his second weapon. But it too remained stuck in the ogre's hair, and so did the sword and the club that followed.

The ogre shook so hard with laughter that all the prince's weapons fell to the ground. "What have you to say now?" he jeered at the prince.

"I was wrong," the young man admitted. "You cannot be conquered with sword and arrows, with club and spear. I must pit myself against you. I shall have to seize you with my bare hands, and crush you to pieces."

"Come on then!" the ogre challenged him.

With a cry Prince Five-Weapons fell upon Sticky-Hair and dealt him a mighty blow with his fist. But his hand remained caught in the hairy coat. Next the prince struck out with his left hand, and this too remained stuck. Then the prince kicked first with his right foot and then with his left. Both feet were trapped as surely as if they had been secured with nails. And finally, the prince struck with his head, and that too was caught in the terrible fur. Prince Five-Weapons could not move at all.

But now the ogre did not laugh at him any more. He said to the prince, "You are a lion among men. Although you are now stuck fast in my hair, helpless and with all your weapons gone, you have not lost your courage. Since I came to live in this forest, no one like you has ever come my way. Can you tell me why you are not afraid?"

"Why should I be afraid?" asked the prince. "After all, each of us is certain to die. And besides, I am not beaten yet."

"But you have no weapons left," the ogre retorted.

"You are mistaken," said Prince Five-Weapons. "My strongest one I have not used so far. Within me is something that would tear you apart if you swallowed me. My fifth weapon lies within me. It is an axe made of rubies, that smites with deadlier force than even a flash of lightning."

"What kind of weapon is that?" asked the terrified monster.

"It is the knowledge of the nature of things," replied Prince Five-Weapons. "That is the all-conquering weapon that my teacher gave me."

The ogre did not know what to reply. He felt afraid of the prince and he let him go. So Prince Five-Weapons continued along the path through the ogre's forest and returned to his home in Benares.

AMERICA

North America

ONE-TWO-MAN AND STONESHIRT

Stoneshirt was a sorcerer who wore a stone shirt which made him invulnerable. Everyone was afraid of him. The Indians never spoke his name aloud, but whispered it: Tump-pwi-nai-ro-gwi-nump. This terrible sorcerer killed people, took women by force and seized whatever he wanted.

One day, he attacked a village where there lived an Indian called the Crane. The sorcerer killed this man and took away his wife. The woman, however, had hidden her young son, so that he was not harmed. The boy was brought up by his grandmother, and she did not speak to him about his parents, because she was too frightened to say the magician's name.

Ten years later, when the lad was sixteen, he was collecting roots one day. All at once, he caught sight of a man sitting beneath a tree. Before the man's feet was a heap of decaying bones. The man looked at the boy with such a penetrating stare that the latter asked, "What do you want of me?"

"It is time to avenge your father," said the man. "It is time to bring back your mother."

"No one has ever mentioned either of them to me. Where is my father?"

The man pointed to the moldering bones. "The sorcerer Stoneshirt killed him."

"And where is my mother?"

"The magician Stoneshirt keeps her a prisoner. He lives by the great lake beyond the mountain. No one has ever dared to seek him out."

"I shall free my mother," said the boy. "I shall avenge my father."

Then the man said, "To be strong enough to defeat Tump-pwi-nai-ro-gwi-nump, there are three things you must do. First you must sleep for four days and four nights. Next, you must get someone to split you in two with your father's axe. And thirdly you must gather your friends and go with them to confront the sorcerer. Will you do these things?"

"I will," the boy promised.

Then the man disappeared and a crane flew up from the spot where the moldy bones were lying. The youth went to his grandmother and told her everything. She listened and said, "It was your father who spoke to you."

The boy slept for four days and four nights. When he

awoke, he was fully grown. He took his father's axe to his grandmother and said, "Split me in two."

At first she refused, but when the Crane's son insisted, she chopped him down the middle. No sooner had she done so when she saw two sons of the Crane before her. So she gave him a new name, One-Two-Man.

One-Two-Man collected his friends about him and they took it as a good sign that they had a double leader. To-go-af the rattlesnake and Shin-au-af the wolf, who were his closest friends, were especially glad and said, "The time has come for Tump-pwi-nai-ro-gwi-nump to tremble."

One-Two-Man went with his friends through the shimmering desert. They climbed the mountain and came to the great lake. Shin-au-af the wolf caught sight of an antelope. "I know who that is," said the wolf. "It is the sorcerer's antelope. It has so many eyes that no one can count them. No one has ever succeeded in getting past it. I shall kill it."

The wolf crept forward towards the antelope, but To-go-af the rattlesnake darted ahead and killed the antelope with a single bite. At first Shin-au-af was annoyed, for he did not like anyone else to get there first. Then he calmed down and together they ate the antelope.

Not far from the village, One-Two-Man met a woman. He knew at once that it was his mother. "I am your son," said One-Two-Man. "I came here to set you free and to avenge my father."

"I have only one son, not two," said the woman.

Then One-Two-Man told her his story and his mother

believed him. But she warned him about Tump-pwi-nai-ro-gwi-nump. "He is invulnerable and his arrows find their target of their own accord."

"Tomorrow he will have no arrows left," said One-Two-Man.

During the night, he crept inside the magician's hut and came out with all the magic arrows. Then To-go-af the rattlesnake crawled into the hut and bit the sorcerer and his three daughters, who were just as cruel as their father.

Next morning, One-Two-Man and his friends were still fast asleep long after sunrise. Shin-au-af the wolf was the first to awaken. He shook One-Two-Man and the rattlesnake awake, and then he roused all the others. "Get up, you lazybones!" said Shin-au-af. "Do you wish to sleep while others do battle with the sorcerer?"

One-Two-Man and the rattlesnake burst into peals of laughter.

"What are you thinking of?" cried Shin-au-af. "Tump-pwi-nai-ro-gwi-nump will hear you!"

"Why not?" asked One-Two-Man.

"Don't worry," the rattlesnake explained. "He can't hear us."

"Because he is dead," said One-Two-Man. "Rattlesnake has bitten him and his three daughters. And I have brought you each a present. An arrow that finds its target by itself."

One-Two-Man held up the bundle of arrows he had taken from the magician's hut. Then his friends stared at him. "Why are you looking at me so?"

"Because there's only one of you again," they said. His mother too asked him, "Weren't there two of you when I met you yesterday?"

He looked down and saw that he was a single person again, now that he had avenged his father and freed his mother from the magician's power. But everyone went on calling him One-Two-Man.

South America

THE FLUTE PLAYER

In ancient times, the boa constrictor was much bigger than it is today. It was also much greedier and used to swallow everything in its path. It was bold enough to devour even tapirs and jaguars. But its favorite food was human flesh. No one was safe from the giant snake.

A mother, two of whose children had already been eaten by the boa, stood up one day in the open air and cried, "What has become of you, warriors? Doesn't our tribe produce men any longer? Come out of your hiding places, you heroes, and go and fight the snake."

The warriors turned a deaf ear. Only one of them, a man who played the flute very well, said, "This woman is right. It's no life for us, when every day is filled with fear."

He slung a knapsack over his shoulder and filled it with toasted maize and he also put in a knife. Then he took his flute and, playing as he went, he left the village behind him.

The boa was attracted by the playing, and crawled along as fast as it could, eager for its prey. The man went on playing as if he had seen nothing. The boa pounced on him and gulped him down.

The man made himself comfortable inside the snake, and prepared for a long stay. He unpacked the toasted maize and the knife. With the latter, he cut off a small piece of the snake's flesh. Because of the pain, the snake blew itself up like a balloon, and the flute player had even more room inside. The boa, however, told all the other giant snakes on no account to swallow people in future, because they could cause such terrible pain.

Piece by piece, the flute player cut away the snake's belly, and when he came to the monster's heart, the boa reared and fell dead. The flute player crept out of the snake. When he returned to his village, he began playing his flute again.

Men, women and children came running up to him, asking, "Where have you been?"

"Inside the great snake," said the man. "Here is a piece of its heart."

Then everyone knew that he had killed the boa.

And since that day, boa constrictors have avoided human beings. They don't want to get stomach aches.

North America

SMOKING STAR

From his earliest days, Smoking Star was famous for his deeds. Indeed, he came into the world in a most unusual way. An old Indian had given his daughter in marriage to a grasping miser and this man tyrannized the whole family. When he shot a bison, he allowed the others to go hungry while he gorged himself with meat. He made his father-in-law act as a beater on bison hunts.

One day, the old man saw a piece of meat lying on the ground, which his son-in-law had overlooked. He picked it up, hid it under his tunic and took it to his wife. She immediately built a fire, set a pot of water to boil, and into the pot she threw the piece of meat. Hardly had the water begun to boil when the old man and his wife heard a child crying. The woman hurriedly took the pot from the fire and looked inside. A child was swimming in the water, crying, "Take me out!"

The woman lifted him out and wrapped him in a blanket. The child slept peacefully all night, and next morning, he said to the old man, "Lift me up and carry me to each of the wigwam poles in turn."

So the old man did as he was bid. Beginning with the pole at the entrance to the wigwam, he walked once around the tent, following the course of the sun. At each pole, the child shot up in height with a jerk. When he had touched only half the wigwam poles, he was already so big that the old man could hardly carry him. At the last one, the boy became a man, and was taller than the old Indian. "Thank you for bringing me to manhood," he said. "My name is Smoking Star. I have come here to perform deeds which will make life easier for you all. Then I shall go away again."

When the old man heard this, he fetched his own weapons and gave them to the young man.

Smoking Star went first to an encampment not far away, and he entered the wigwam of three old women. They were surprised that such a handsome young man came to visit them. "Why do you come to us, rather than go with the young people?" they asked him. He left the question unanswered and asked for nothing but a small piece of dried meat. Each of the three gave him a piece of dried meat, but no fat with it.

"You are very kind to me," said Smoking Star, "but you might have given me a little fat to go with the dried meat."

"Hush," said the women, "not so loud. There are bears about who have eaten all our fat. They will kill you if they hear you speak like that. They fill the neighborhood with terror."

"If that is so, we shall kill bison tomorrow. Then we shall have some fat!"

Smoking Star made his way through the camp, inviting all the men to take part in a bison hunt the next day. He offered to drive the bison towards the camp, and this he did so well that the hunters were able to shoot a large number of them. They were fat beasts too, as everyone saw when the carcasses were cut up. The fat was hung in strips from long poles. The bears smelled it at once and came down from their haunts to steal the fat for themselves. They were huge animals with terrible paws—twelve giants, the biggest bears in the world.

Meanwhile, Smoking Star had built a fire in which he heated a large number of stones. The fire provoked the bears' anger. And when Smoking Star removed the fat from the poles and wrapped it up, the bears were furious. Their leader and its mate fell upon Smoking Star with open jaws. But Smoking Star threw hot stones into their gaping mouths, and both bears choked to death. The other bears fled. Smoking Star pursued them to their lair and killed them all, except for one she-bear that was in cub. She looked at him so pleadingly that he allowed her to live.

And so the race of bears was preserved from extinction. But from that time on, the Indian tribe could keep all the fat they needed. Smoking Star gave the three old women a big supply. He also rescued a young girl, whom the bears had carried off and had kept as a prisoner in their hide-out.

Next, Smoking Star headed for a place which was infested with snakes. He killed them all, except for one female, which was ready to produce its young. Thus the snake species was also saved from extinction.

Beside the lake ran a path, but no one had been able to use it for some time. For the traveler would be seized by a powerful whirlwind, which carried him into the mouth of an enormous fish. This was the Great Sucker Fish, and the whirlwind was its tremendous suction.

Smoking Star walked along this dangerous path. He was seized by the whirlwind and whisked inside the fish. There were many people in its belly, but most of them were dead. To the survivors, Smoking Star said, "Somewhere inside this fish there must be a heart. Let us dance around it."

He had recognized the fish's heart immediately. It hung above the captives menacingly.

Smoking Star painted his face white and drew black lines round his eyes and mouth. Then he firmly tied a sharp stone knife to his forehead, so that the knife tip jutted out like a horn. Some of the people carried rattles made of stag's hoofs, and they began to shake them. The others danced in the middle with Smoking Star. At first he jumped no higher than a goat, and he waved his arms as an eagle flaps its wings. Then gradually he leaped higher and higher until the stone knife pierced the heart of the Great Sucker Fish. Now it was dead, and it drifted to the shore where it was washed up. Smoking Star cut a door in the great fish's side, and all those who were still alive were able to leave safely.

Soon after this, Smoking Star met a giant ogress. She would not allow anyone to pass unless he wrestled with her first. But no one had ever wrestled with her and lived.

"You are the man everyone is talking about," she said. "Now show me if you are stronger than I."

"I have been traveling for ten hours," Smoking Star answered. "Let me rest a little first."

As he rested, he looked around him very carefully. He saw that there were tips of pointed knives showing through a layer of straw. The handles had been stuck in the ground.

"Aha," thought Smoking Star. "So that's her trick. As they wrestle, she throws her opponent so that he falls with his back on the knives." Then he said to the ogress, "I am quite rested now." So the wrestling match began. Smoking Star allowed himself to be steered to the spot that was bristling with knives. The ogress was already confident of her victory, when Smoking Star made a lightning throw and flung her with her back on the knives. So the ogress died, not Smoking Star.

His last deed was performed beside a swift river with steep banks. A cunning old woman lived nearby, and she had erected a swing which had very long ropes. She was having a swing herself as Smoking Star came by, and as usual with travelers, she told him to try the swing. Smoking Star saw at once that a trap had been laid, and he asked her first if she would show him how the swinging was done. He pushed the swing several times for her, so that she swung far out over the rushing waters. Then suddenly he cut through one of the ropes, just as the old woman had done with all her previous victims. Now it was her turn to fly through the air and into the river, where she was drowned.

After this adventure, Smoking Star went back to the place he had come from. He chose a path that led through the land of the Cree Indians. He died uncomplaining, struck by their arrows.

Mexico

UITZITON AND THE FIRST QUARREL

The original home of the Aztecs was a place called Aztlan. When their numbers had increased greatly, Aztlan became too cramped for them. But they did not dare to move elsewhere, because there had been no sign from heaven.

One of their chiefs was named Uitziton. He was a brave man and a clever one. As he sat one day lost in thought, he heard a bird that kept calling, "Tiui-tiui! Tiui-tiui!" In the language of the Aztecs, that meant, "Go forth, go forth!"

Uitziton discussed this with Tecpatzin, who was equally respected by the people. Uitziton thought, "It is easier for two of us to convince the people than one." And that was how it happened. When the bird call was heard again, Uitziton said to the people, "Listen everybody! Listen to what the bird is saying!"

"Go forth, go forth! That is what it is calling," said Tecpatzin.

"Yes," said many of them. "It is calling 'tiui-tiui!' "

"It is a sign from heaven," declared Uitziton. "We have heard it."

"Heaven has sent us a sign," nodded Tecpatzin.

Then many men and women, together with their children, agreed to leave Aztlan, and the future of the Aztec people was assured.

Long before this, Uitziton had sent out scouts, so he knew where there was a land in which they could settle and thrive.

But not far from Aztlan, there was a sinister spot which was known as the Snake's Jaws. It was the home of an evil spirit, who tried to harm the Aztecs at every opportunity.

When this spirit observed that the Aztecs were about to part in peace and harmony, he decided to inveigle them into a dispute. He crept into the camp in the dead of night, and left two bundles on the ground. At daybreak, these bundles were discovered. Everyone pushed and jostled to see them. Eagerly, someone opened the first bundle. There came to light an incredibly large emerald, a jewel of incalculable value.

"It belongs to us who are leaving," said some.

"No, it belongs to us who are staying," insisted others.

"To us, who are going to found a new home!" cried some.

"To us, who keep faith with the old country!" shouted others.

The quarrel grew more and more violent. Then Uitziton stepped forward and held up the other bundle, which everyone had forgotten in the uproar. "You hotheads!" he cried. "Why are you quarreling over a stone? First let us see what is in the other bundle."

That calmed the shouting throng and they craned their necks as Uitziton unwrapped the other bundle. Two sticks came into sight, a round one and a flat one. A murmur of disappointment ran through the crowd.

Uitziton, however, realized that what he held in his hands was worth more than any jewel. To those who were leaving with him, he said, "Leave the emerald here. These two pieces of wood will be much more useful to us on our long march!"

On the trek into the new land, it was shown what a good exchange Uitziton had made when he chose the two sticks instead of the emerald. At the first halt, everyone felt frozen with the cold. So Uitziton brought out the two sticks, placed the round one in the hole in the flat one, and twirled the stick between his palms until the lower end of the round stick began to burn. Now the people had fire and everyone could warm themselves beside it.

THE SEVEN DEEDS OF ONKOITO

Onkoito lived with both his grandfathers on top of a cliff. The cliff was a dangerous place, for it was the home of a chipmunk. The chipmunk used to appear out of the blue, as if offering itself as a target. But if anyone went out to capture the chipmunk, he would find himself surrounded by rattlesnakes. In this manner, Onkoito's grandfathers had lost three of their sons.

In the same neighborhood there lived a chief named Sawhorse. He used to arrange dancing festivals for his tribe, and when others arrived out of curiosity, the dancers fell upon the strangers and killed them. Two of the grandfathers' sons had died in this way.

Somewhat farther afield lived an old woman. She was known as the-woman-who-straightens-men's-backs, for when passers-by called on her, she would insist on massaging their backs for them. Then as they lay there, she would break their spines with a heavy pounder.

There was also a wapiti who roamed the district, making fools of its hunters. Whoever chased it was lured on and on, until he died of exhaustion. Yet no one had ever seen the wapiti face to face. But because of the-woman-who-straightens-men's-backs and the wapiti whom no one ever saw, Onkoito's grandfathers lost two more of their sons.

One day, the two grandfathers with four of their sons made an expedition to the southwest, in order to shoot wild geese. When they halted to cook some food and eat it, there was a rushing sound overhead. A sea-eagle, bigger than any they had ever seen before, swooped down on them. The sons sprang to their feet and shot their arrows, but they missed. The great bird of prey killed them all with its talons. So the grandfathers returned home to their three surviving sons.

One day, these three sons went to a river where a strange plant grew, not far from the rapids. The sons swam out to the flower to pick it, but two were drowned beneath the rapids. The third reached the far bank, but he could not pluck the flower.

Now on this bank stood a sweat-lodge, where the men used to gather to amuse themselves with gambling. Outside there were women treading acorns for acorn soup, which the gamblers liked to eat. A steep slope led from the lodge entrance to the gaming-room below, and its floor was as smooth as glass. Many people slipped on it and fell to their deaths, including Onkoito's last uncle.

The grandfathers had only one daughter. When they told her of the deaths of the last three sons, she left the house weeping. Suddenly a man stood beside her and he said, "You would do better to marry me instead of weeping. I am the Cloud Man."

The daughter liked the Cloud Man, and so she became his wife.

One day, the Cloud Man said, "I must go away. But you will bear two children. Call one of them Pemsauto, Never-Satisfied, for he will eat a great deal of food. The other you must call Onkoito, the Conqueror, for he will accomplish seven great deeds."

Then the Cloud Man went away. The woman gave birth to two sons and she called them Pemsauto and Onkoito. Pemsauto became a glutton, and Onkoito became a great hunter. The two grandfathers worried about their grandchildren, for they had lost all their own sons.

When the chipmunk called from the cliff, the grandfathers warned Onkoito, "Don't go near the cliff, it is a bad place. Three of our sons lost their lives there."

But Onkoito shot the chipmunk. Then he put on stone shoes and went to fetch it. As the rattlesnakes darted out, he trampled them underfoot.

"None of them will bite you any more," said Onkoito, and he brought home the chipmunk he had killed. The grandfathers danced for joy and said, "You have avenged three of our sons."

A week later, Onkoito visited Chief Sawhorse. He was

dancing at the sweat-lodge with others of his tribe. "Do come in, Onkoito!" called the chief in a loud voice. As the young man entered, the others set on him to kill him. But he flailed them with his fists, so that they all went flying. They were so panic-stricken that they could not find the way out and they trampled each other to death.

The grandfathers praised Onkoito. "Two more sons have been avenged. That makes five in all."

The very next day, Onkoito went to see the-woman-who-straightens-men's-backs. "What a pity your back is crooked," said the old woman to Onkoito. "Your mother should have straightened it when you were born. But never mind. I can still put it right for you, if you like."

"More than anything," said Onkoito, and lay down full length on the smooth rock. The old woman began to massage Onkoito with the palms of her hands. Suddenly she reached behind her for the pounder with which she broke her victim's spine. So swiftly did Onkoito throw himself to one side that the pounder hit the rock and was shattered to fragments. One sharp stone splinter pierced the woman's heart, and she fell dead on the spot.

On the way home, Onkoito encountered the wapiti. He chased after it but the wapiti gave a great leap and hid itself in a crack between two clouds. Onkoito shot it with an arrow and as the clouds parted, the mysterious animal fell to the ground. Onkoito carried it home as a trophy.

"You have avenged another two sons," said the grandfathers. "That makes seven in all."

When Onkoito set out on his next adventure, the grandfathers went with him. Never-Satisfied joined them as soon as he had eaten half the wapiti. They traveled south and they shot many ducks.

As they were roasting the ducks, there was a rushing noise overhead and the big sea-eagle swooped. Pemsauto was busy with the cooking for he intended to eat at least six ducks himself. But the grandfathers threw stones at the eagle, and Onkoito shattered its skull.

"Four more sons have you avenged!" cried the grandfathers. "That makes eleven now."

Then Onkoito said, "All I have to do now is to avenge the ones who tried to swim the river, and the last of my uncles who went to the sweat-lodge where men gamble all day. Will you come with me?"

The two grandfathers agreed at once, but Pemsauto wanted to go home first, for half the wapiti had not yet been eaten. But when he heard there was acorn soup at the sweat-lodge, he changed his mind and went with the others.

The grandfathers and Pemsauto were the first to swim the river, but they kept their distance from the flower, for they were frightened of the rapids. But Onkoito struck out boldly. He plucked the flower and carried it to the opposite bank.

In front of the sweat-lodge there were women trampling acorns, and others were making acorn soup. But inside the lodge, gaming was in full swing. Onkoito broke sticks of cane for the grandfathers and his brother. By leaning on these sticks, the three were able to enter the gambling den without falling to their deaths. Onkoito, however, was wearing his heavy stone shoes and he began dancing on the glassy floor. So wildly did he dance that before long, the surface was broken to pieces.

"Now we shall see who wins at games of chance," said Onkoito to the players who were already there. The newcomers quickly saw that the others were cheats and thorough-going scoundrels who would stop at nothing as long as they won. They did not even take time out to eat the acorn soup that the women brought them. Only Pemsauto ate and ate, until there was none left. The players watched closely, expecting to see Pemsauto burst, he ate so much, but Never-Satisfied could digest any amount of food.

"And now," cried Onkoito," we'll play without cheating!" The men jumped to their feet. Suddenly they had weapons in their hands.

Then Onkoito sang the Great Song of the North Wind. And the North Wind came clattering down on the players and they all froze. The icy cold penetrated their hearts and killed those unscrupulous cheats.

The grandfathers were proud of their grandson Onkoito. "Now you have avenged all our sons," they said. "Long will people tell the tale of how we won the game."

Then they all went home.

North America

NORWAN

Norwan, the Woman of the South, lived with her brother Hessiha on the hill called Norwan Buli.

Olelbis, "the one above," had made her the most beautiful of women. He had stretched out his hand to the southeast and plucked a yosan flower so that Norwan should have a staff for dancing such as no one had ever possessed before. Olelbis had put two blue feathers in her hair and rubbed her cheeks with red blossoms. Finally he had bestowed on her the gift of dancing more beautifully than any other woman. Sometimes Norwan would dance from morning till night.

Tales of Norwan's beauty were told everywhere and many young men wanted her for a wife. One after the other they came to Hessiha to woo the Woman of the South.

"Sedit has been to see me," said Hessiha to Norwan. "He's a good man and he asked for your hand in marriage. Will you be his wife?"

"I'd rather marry a beaver," laughed Norwan. "Sedit's breath smells."

"Puyuk has been to see me," said Hessiha to Norwan. "He's a good man. Will you marry him?"

"I'd rather marry a bear," laughed Norwan. "Puyuk's legs are as thin as a crane's and he doesn't know how to dance."

"Herit has been to see me. He's a good man," said Hessiha. "Will you be his wife?"

"I'd rather marry a coyote," laughed Norwan. "Herit's nose is like a moccasin."

"Helina has been to see me," said Hessiha. "He's a good man. Will you be his wife?"

"I'd rather marry a bison," said Norwan, laughing. "Helina stinks like pitch."

"And then, Norbis has been to see me too. He's a good man," said Hessiha. "Will you be his wife?"

"Let Norbis come," said Norwan.

"Why do you want to marry Norbis?" asked Hessiha.

"Because he is destined for me," said the Woman of the South.

So Norbis came and Norwan married him. For three years they lived happily together. Then one day, she received an invitation to a grand feast. Norwan was seized with a great longing to dance and she said to her husband, "Shall we accept this invitation?"

"I know how much dancing means to you," said Norbis. "Of course we'll go."

So Norwan decked herself out for the feast and wherever she passed on her way to the dance, people said, "Look, here comes Norwan. No one is as beautiful as she."

The Tsudi girls who also wanted to go to the feast, implored her, "Tell us what to wear! You know best!"

And Norwan dressed them for the dance. She arrayed them from head to foot, and put yellow and red feathers in their hair. And she did it all so skillfully that it took but a moment. The same thing happened with the Patkili young men. Norwan decked them out too and they caught her passion for the dance.

Now the Redbreast brothers were also invited to the dance. They were the most famous dancers among all the Wintu Indians. When they saw Norwan dancing, they would dance with no one else. And as she danced with the Redbreast brothers, Norwan forgot everything, even her brother Hessiha and Norbis, her husband. She danced away with the two Redbreast brothers and they all disappeared into the night.

When they did not return, Norbis went home to Norwan Buli and told Hessiha what had happened. "Go to the Redbreast brothers," said Norbis. "Tell them that your sister must return to me. If they do not send her back, there will be war between us. For her absence is an insult not only to me, but to the whole tribe."

Hessiha did as he was bid and said to the Redbreast brothers, "I must speak to my sister Norwan. I have a message for her from her husband."

One of the brothers went into the house, but he came out again, saying, "I have a message from Norwan. She refuses to acknowledge either her husband or her brother."

"Bring her here," said Hessiha angrily, "or blood will flow."

The Redbreast brothers refused to go, saying, "Norwan is her own mistress."

"Then ask her if she wants to see many men killed for her sake," said Hessiha.

The second Redbreast brother went indoors and came out again saying, "Norwan says that all she wants is to dance. If people go to war, that is none of her business."

"There will be war," repeated Hessiha. "There will be war on this woman's account." And filled with sadness, he returned to Norbis.

Norbis called his friends together. More than one hundred came at his request. "The Redbreast brothers refuse to give me back my wife," he said to them. "They have insulted me."

"Then they have insulted us too," said his friends.

They gathered all their allies together and prepared to wage war. The Redbreast brothers did the same.

In the battles that followed, the braves on both sides performed deeds of incredible heroism. In the end, half the men were killed and the others were either wounded or completely exhausted. Norbis, Hessiha and the Redbreast brothers all withdrew, each to his own side. No one had won.

One day, Norwan appeared at the house where her husband and brother lived. When they came out to see who had arrived, Norwan said, "Now I know that it was all my fault. It was because of me that so many people died."

"What do you want now?" asked her brother Hessiha.

"I don't know," said Norwan.

"Come in," said Norbis, leading her by the hand into the house.

"Why are you doing that?" asked Hessiha.

"Because she has come back," said Norbis.

South America

AFTER THE GREAT FIRE

A long time ago, there was a war in the Land of the Yurakara that dragged on and on. First they fought with slings and stones, then with spears and poisoned arrows. At last, there set in a time of great drought, and Sararuma, an evil spirit who hated all mankind, gave both sides a piece of advice. He told them to set fire to the grasslands and the forests. A great blaze raced through the land. In their passion to destroy each other, the people did not recognize Sararuma, and so they all died.

Only one man had refused to take part in the slaughter. He had dug himself a deep pit, for he had foreseen how it would end. He and his wife hid themselves deep in the earth, and so they were spared. After the great fire, they were the only human beings left alive.

After some time, the man held up his arm and poked a long twig out of the pit. When he looked at it, he saw the tip was burning.

The next day he tried again, and for the second time the twig burst into flame. Then the man tried on each of the next three days, and when at last the twig did not catch fire, the man climbed out of his hiding place.

"What can you see?" his wife asked him.

"Ashes," he said.

The woman climbed out of the pit and saw that everything was burned black. No grass or trees were left, no people and no animals. Suddenly Sararuma appeared before them wearing a cloak as red as flame.

"Do you want to go on living in this black wilderness?" Sararuma taunted them.

"Yes," said the man, and his wife nodded.

Then Sararuma started shrinking. Grass sprouted from the ashes.

"I tell you the earth will be consumed by fire again," shouted Sararuma. "Consider well if you really wish to go on living."

"Yes, we want to go on living," said the wife.

Then the charred trees began turning green. Sararuma dwindled to half his size.

"You're the last survivors," he said maliciously. "You'll have no one else to talk to."

"Things will change," said the man. And his wife added, "We shall have children."

Then animals rose from the ashes, and Sararuma was turned into a gust of wind that was blown away, howling.

Hans Baumann was born in Bavaria in 1914. He taught school there and later turned to writing for young people.

Mr. Baumann is the author of a number of highly acclaimed and widely translated books on archeology and early cultures. These include *The Caves of the Great Hunters, Gold and Gods of Peru, The World of the Pharaohs,* and *In the Land of Ur,* winner of the Mildred L. Batchelder Award.

Mr. Baumann lives in Murnau, Germany.

Baumann, Hans, 1914-
The stolen fire; legends of heroes and rebels from around the world. Translated by Stella Humphries. Illustrated by Herbert Holzing. [New York] Pantheon Books [c1974]
150 p. illus.

1. Tales. I. Title.